Prince Regent

Prince Regent
is based on scripts
from the BBC television
serial by

ROBERT MULLER
NEMONE LETHBRIDGE
DAVID TURNER
IAN CURTEIS
and
REG GADNEY

JOHN BURKE

Prince Regent

Based on the BBC serial originated by

IAN AND JOAN CURTEIS

FONTANA / COLLINS

First published in 1979 by Fontana Paperbacks

Made and printed in Great Britain by
William Collins Sons & Co Ltd Glasgow

CONTENTS

PART ONE

FLORIZEL

CHAPTER ONE

On a sunny July afternoon in 1784 George Augustus Frederick, Prince of Wales, sat in his garden beside the cascade and wept. It was a habit of his. He would have sworn that he and his disagreeable father had nothing whatsoever in common, but in fact they were alike in this: at the slightest excuse both King George III and his eldest son wept copious tears – at the sound of Handel's music, the murmur of a woman's voice, the threat of a quarrel brewing or the promise of a maudlin reconciliation. Hatred and remorse were equally capable of tickling the tear ducts. And, in this case, desire.

The Prince of Wales wanted Mrs Maria Fitzherbert in his arms and in his bed. She smiled at him most adorably; but refused to succumb. He had offered his heart, the vision of a richly rewarding future, and an unceasing flow of gifts; but she was a virtuous widow and would be no man's mistress. So he cried, declared he would worship her until his dying day, and threatened to bring that day closer.

Once before he had sent for a succession of surgeons to bleed him so that he might present a pale appearance and melt her resolve. Calling at her house in Park Street he had let himself stagger helplessly in the hope that she would put her arms round him. When there was no reaction other than that calm, gently affectionate smile, he had cried out reproachfully:

'Madam, regard me! I am sick with love.'

'You'll recover.'

'I have become much emaciated.'

'It becomes you.'

'I have contracted a violent cough.'

'Your physician will doubtless prescribe the appropriate cure.'

'This very morning I have spat blood, madam.'

'Then it behoves you to repudiate all excitements, does it not?'

She allowed him to follow her into her drawing-room, and sat demurely facing him. Truly his heart did beat faster and he did feel faint. How should he not, confronted by such a superb, incomparable woman? There were some who, not at first knowing of his feelings for her, had commented in his hearing that she was a trifle large, somewhat matronly for her age, and her nose was more than a trifle too long. Which proved their appalling lack of taste. Maria Fitzherbert was a goddess: a celestial being whose skin glowed with an inner radiance, whose hair was a veritable halo, like no mortal hair. There was a scent from her shoulders – on the rare occasions she allowed him close enough – which intoxicated. And always there was that unflirtatious yet affectionate smile, the smile of a fond aunt indulging an impetuous little boy. He was sure that affection could turn to love if she would only let it.

Yet she spoke only absurdities such as, 'I am too old for you, my friend.' Too old? What was a mere six years? He was twenty-two, he wanted no inexperienced chit of a girl. Maria's dignity and wisdom, acquired from her two late husbands: these were what he most needed and most admired.

'Too old?' Seated in his garden, bending wretchedly forward so that tears splashed on to his white breeches, he heard his own voice resonating on in his head. 'You mean too virtuous,' he had accused her.

'I could never consent to be your mistress,' she had gravely confessed.

What was to be done? She meant more to him than anyone had ever done or ever could do. He had but one desire. He would not be thwarted. She must listen.

George lurched to his feet and turned towards the house.

For once he paid no heed to the splendours of the garden on which so much care had been lavished. He walked without so much as a glance past the Chinese silks which his trusted Henry Holland had so imaginatively hung in the salon. All the brightness irradiating Carlton House would remain for him darkness, unless Maria would condescend to share it with him.

At the end of the corridor he stopped before a mirror framed in tendrils and curlicues of beaten gold. Was he not tolerably handsome? Some might have found his lower lip too full; but it was admirable for kissing. His sash was tight, and two of the padded buttons on his plum-coloured velvet jacket were straining somewhat; but he was tall enough to carry a certain amount of weight, and there was nothing which his tailor could not fix in an hour or two.

Were his liquid, yearning eyes not irresistible in their honesty?

Mrs Fitzherbert, alas, seemed well able to resist. So all the magnificence of his Carlton House setting had become tawdry, and he himself was as unreal as that sad image in its gilt-laden glass.

He turned resolutely away from that phantom, carried his sword up to his bedroom, and unsheathed it.

The first tentative scratch on his bared arm made him wince. With an effort he attempted a deeper cut, but could not bring himself to saw down with the blade. Tearing open his shirt, he tried to force the point into his ample stomach, but again flinched away. A little bubble of blood winked at him. He must do it. He must prove his determination to leave this world forever, so that she should see how she had wronged him.

Closing his eyes, he leaned forward, let out a howl as the blade drove into him, and managed to twist himself over it so that blood began to gush and flow more freely.

Then he reached for the bell-pull and tugged it frantically.

'Your Royal Highness . . .'

'I have fallen on my sword. I'm in agony. Fetch a surgeon. Fetch Keate.'

The two servants whimpered in disbelief. Did they suppose he was only play-acting? Or could they not accept that the Prince of Wales was at death's door?

He let the sword clatter to the floor and clutched his hands over the bloody smears on his stomach and shirt.

'Fetch Mrs Fitzherbert!'

Then he fell back on the bed.

Oh, this was no histrionic gesture. He was sincere. Child and man, had he not always been utterly sincere? Sincere in seeking only the best: in wanting to be the finest soldier – which his pompous father forbade him to be; the greatest patron of the arts this unappreciative country could ever hope for – an expenditure which aroused his father's fury; and the truest, most honest lover of the finest and truest woman in the world – of whom his father had so far heard only a few disquieting rumours.

He had always been straight and true, had he not?

CHAPTER TWO

Of course there had been Mary Hamilton, that girl at Court attending on his innumerable sisters. It had to be admitted that he had written her a most poetic letter, and won from her a locket containing a strand of her hair and bearing the inscription *Toujours Aimée*. But he had been not quite seventeen at the time, and of course it had never been a serious affair, and no harm came of it. And as for Perdita . . .

Oh, Mary Robinson, his Perdita. 'Oh, Mrs Robinson,' he had sighed. And sighed and sighed until she fell into his arms.

Such a very beautiful actress, and so entrancing as Perdita in *The Winter's Tale* that what else could he be but her Florizel? He had been sincere, though in the end she had not proved worthy of him. It had been a two-year delight, a breathless game of secret meetings in the garden of the little castellated palace at Kew, of a gossamer figure drifting across moonlit grass to become yielding flesh in his rooms, of exploration and ecstasy. But she was, after all, only a girl: married and with a baby, but not the kind of experienced wife or widow he craved. And so deplorably vindictive when the end came. When in all good faith he had decided it was time to discard her because he was experiencing new and less arduous pleasures with Mrs Armistead, the mistress his obliging friend Fox had loaned him, the ethereal Perdita began to make vengeful noises. How could one so exquisite be so coarse about matters like the money he had promised to settle on her, the position he had promised her in his household when he came of age, the many lighthearted things he had said in his letters?

It had cost his father £5000 to buy back those letters

before they were published for the whole country to read.

George III did not like parting with money. It was one of the many bones of contention between them. The King believed his son should lead a frugal, industrious life. To this end he had ordered him to be regularly thrashed by his tutors, lectured on the moral issues which those of royal lineage must sustain, and exhorted to spend no penny on vain show or entertainment; and had ignored all George's pleas that he should be allowed to take up a command in the army, to travel, to have an establishment of his own.

At eighteen it was widely agreed, especially among the Prince's friends, that he ought to be able to live away from Buckingham House and away from his father's permanently critical eye. King George thought exactly the opposite. He hated those friends such as Charles James Fox and Richard Brinsley Sheridan who not only derided the Prince's father for losing the American colonies but urged the Whigs to treat amiably with the rebels, and were all too clearly only waiting for the day when their drinking and gambling companion should himself become King. His father meant to keep young George waiting – a long time for the succession, and as long as possible for an establishment of his own.

But as the Prince's twenty-first birthday approached, in the year when those Americans were concluding their successful war of independence, influential voices in Parliament urged that he must be granted an increased allowance and a suitable home. The King argued; but gave in. He would pay a personal allowance to his son, and with Parliament's help Carlton House above the Mall should be fitted up for him. It was not so very far from Buckingham House: not far enough to deprive the King of knowledge of the Prince's doings.

It did not take long for a new series of conflicts to break out.

'Corinthian porticoes? Colonnades? How much is this damned house going to cost by the time you've finished, eh, what-what?'

This opening broadside was fired in the King's drawing-room at Windsor. George had been summoned to ride down with his favourite brother, Frederick, Duke of York. Neither had known what to expect, but George tried to look on the bright side and assure himself that his father, having seen reason about Carlton House, was now going to relent on the question of a military appointment.

Facing the King, the Prince learnt he had been over-optimistic.

'Rebuilding the confounded place, what? A touch of paint, that's all it needed. Some paint and a few sticks of furniture. Additions where necessary, I told you. Where necessary!'

'Father, as a connoisseur of the Arts I found it necessary to — '

'The Arts, what-what? Do the Arts include frills and furbelows and . . . and gambling, dissipation, tailoring . . .?' The King flourished a sheaf of bills as if to shower them across the room.

Frederick glanced wryly at his brother.

Before George could speak, the King went on: 'But no matter. That is not what I wish to talk about today.'

George tried to repress too obvious a sigh of relief. 'I'm grateful to your Majesty.'

'The subject is your appeals for careers in the Army. Both of you.'

'Majesty knows how long I have yearned to serve my country. I have ever regarded it as my most urgent task.'

'Your most urgent task, sir, is to prepare yourself to be King of England. To show that the anxious care I have lavished upon you has not been misspent.' Again the sheaf of bills was waved in denunciation. 'Not wasted on debauchery with idle companions, men of no principle, women of . . . eh, what-what? You show, if I may say so, few signs of responsibility.'

'You give me few opportunities to *display* responsibility, sir.'

'You neglect your studies. Always did. Your German is as clumsy as your Latin.'

This was carrying things too far. 'My Latin is excellent,' said George proudly. 'As for my German, I shall perfect it whilst serving in Hanover.'

'You will not be serving in Hanover.'

'But I thought . . . from what you were saying, Papa . . .'

'You are not going to Hanover.' The King turned to his second and favourite son. 'Frederick is to be the soldier. It is decided.'

The Duke of York could not this time meet his brother's gaze. He gulped, and drew himself up to attention.

'But I . . .' George fumbled for words to express the impossible. 'I'm not even permitted to complete my military education? For what reasons?'

'For reasons of your extravagance, sir, which have for so long been trumpeted in the public prints.'

'Those same prints, I take it' – George snarled it out with no heed for the respect on which his father was always so insistent – 'which show you, sir, as a weak fool who has lost us our American possessions in less time than it takes to turn out a decent pair of boots?'

King George turned away. The audience was at an end.

The Prince felt a moment of bitter envy against his brother. But it did not last. They had always been so close, always fought and played and gone wenching together. He could not cease to love Frederick.

'While we're here,' Frederick was saying warily, 'I think you ought to go and see mother. You've neglected her of late.'

To go and see mother! With her piety and droning lectures, even worse than his father's, and all those children about her whose names he could never remember. Adolphus Frederick, Ernest Augustus, Sophia Augusta, Octavius, and now this new little creature – how should he possibly memorize all his brothers and sisters or know one from another? It was disgusting that she should continue producing in this fashion, adding more and more claims on an exchequer which might be so much better employed by the one rightful heir.

George stormed back to London and sought out Henry Holland.

'His Majesty hates me, has hated me all my life. So be it. Now, Mr Holland, let's give him cause for his displeasure. The Corinthian porticoes, for a start.'

'I may proceed?'

'Proceed, Mr Holland. I intend Carlton House to be the most perfect palace in Europe. The envy of the world. The Ionic colonnade – no more delays. And I demand balustraded wings, the main hall is to be paved in marble – Italian marble, mark you — '

'The cost, Royal Highness — '

'Will, I trust, be enormous. All the tin mines in my Duchy of Cornwall will not pay a quarter. I want a lasting monument, Mr Holland, to your skill and my taste.'

If he could not serve in the Army, must not leave the country, must not do this or that to prove his worth, how *might* he employ his time? By commissioning a bathroom fit for a Roman consul, a conservatory in Gothic style in which to feast a thousand friends for an unbroken week.

And by seeking a companion worthy of his love and manhood.

Looking back, it was all too plain that none of his amorous adventures had been on the same high plane as his aesthetic aspirations. There had been an earlier Maria, the diverting Countess of Salisbury. And Lady Melbourne, whose husband so appropriately became Gentleman of the Bedchamber to the Prince of Wales. And the flirtatious Mrs Hodges, and Lady Effingham, and the persevering Countess of Hardenburg. But these had been merely diversions. Once he met Mrs Fitzherbert he knew he had met his fate.

It had happened at a dull reception where his father had insisted on playing the harpsichord – badly, as usual.

And then they had chanced to meet at the Opera, and in that immediate vision of her loveliness he saw the grace of a Raphael, the serenity of a Botticelli – and, in her serene amplitude, the sweetly fleshy promise of a Rubens.

Yet here he was now, his life's blood draining away, because she would not yield.

'Where is Mrs Fitzherbert?'

The surgeon stemming his wound tried to hold him down on the bed. 'If you will lie still, your Royal Highness . . .'

'Send Colonel Lake. If he cannot fetch Mrs Fitzherbert to me, all your attentions will be in vain, my dear Keate.'

Lake took so long to find the lady that George began to worry about his symptoms. The bleeding had been staunched, he had been washed and powdered and given a resuscitatory draught, and was fair to recover before she arrived to witness what he had endured. He tore at the bandages to reopen the wound.

When at last Lake brought her to his bed of pain, the Prince heard the murmured explanations.

'His Royal Highness was distraught . . . determined to proceed . . . promised . . . threatened . . .'

'Neither promises nor threats can be entirely reliable,' said that beloved voice, 'when offered in such an extravagant manner.'

No matter. There she was beside his bed with that same forever tolerant smile, that slightly disdainful but always amused look down her gaunt nose. The green silk that went so well with the faintly auburn gloss of her hair asked to be stroked; but its texture could be no softer than the sweetness of her skin.

George raised himself gallantly on one elbow.

'It's you, my beloved. You have come . . . just in time.'

'My dear . . .' Oh, at least she had called him her dear! 'I came on the insistence of your equerry. I did not wish you to suffer further injury.' She looked sceptically at the twisted bandages. 'But now I see that you merely make sport of me.'

'Never! Maria, my angel, I conjure you from the most profound depths of my heart. Best and most adored of women, come and crown with bliss the one who'll convince you by his love that he is the best of husbands — '

'A husband?'

'But what else? What else, my dearest of wives?'

'It is not possible. And you know it.'

He heaved himself out of bed and collapsed on his knees, tearing his hair. Could she not see the agony he was in, physical and mental? I will forgo the throne, sell all my possessions, abandon this country . . . Was he saying that aloud or was it simply pulsing through his mind? He held out his hand imploringly; then remembered that there was a ring, that he had put it away against such a moment, that she must believe in the reality of a gold ring. Through a mist of tears he saw the embarrassed Colonel Lake, trying to turn away yet having nothing else on which plausibly to fix his attention.

'Lake, the ring.'

'Your Royal Highness?'

George waved a desperate hand at the upper drawer of his bedside cabinet. His equerry opened it, scrabbled within, and brought out the plain gold band.

'Forgive me, Maria.' The Prince's voice was choked with sobs. 'I have never presumed to make you any offer with a view to . . . to purchasing your virtue. You must see how true I am, how true all my intentions.'

She blurred across his vision. To his amazement, and with the beginnings of joy, he realized that she, too, was weeping.

She sank into a chair, protesting: 'You're not dying, or even ill. You're acting.'

'No. I will prove it. We'll flee together. Now, tomorrow. To France, to Hanover . . .'

'There's no need' – she controlled her tears better than

he could – 'to go to such unconscionable lengths of passion. I have no desire to destroy either my own tranquillity or yours.'

'You will marry me?'

The stricken equerry backed away as far as possible, longing to be out of earshot.

Maria raised glowing yet unhappy eyes below the fine crown of her hair. 'I would have to ask that whatever document you saw fit to draw up would satisfy both my conscience and my Church.'

'You're saying yes?'

'I . . .'

He reached out and seized her hand, forcing the ring on to her finger. Mrs Fitzherbert stared at it, gently shaking her head; then rose with a grace more regal than his mother or any of his sisters dare ever hope to match.

'We will talk again tomorrow,' she said, 'when you are recovered.'

The loss of blood and the anguish of his passion had drained him utterly. He was exhausted; but content. He had won. She would be his.

'Tomorrow,' he said into the middle of a roseate dream.

On that hoped-for morrow he learned that she had hastily shut up her Park Street house and left for Dover, on her way to France, announcing that she had no intention of returning for some considerable time.

CHAPTER THREE

'She must come back. And I must make her my wife.'

Charles James Fox lolled in the armchair he favoured when visiting the Prince. His eyes were half closed, but this apparent somnolence was deceptive: below those heavy, dark, sardonic eyebrows he was shrewdly observant – and worried.

'At the risk of displeasing you,' he ventured, 'you must *not*.'

'I have decided, Charles.'

'You can't. She's a Catholic.'

'What matters that to me?'

'It matters to the people,' said Fox. 'The nation is prejudiced.'

'But I am not.'

Fox moodily held out his glass as a flunkey came in with a replenished decanter. When the man had left, he took a long draught and said tersely:

'Your children will be bastards.'

George had hoped for better from his old crony. They had dined so often together and gambled so often until the small hours; shared many a bottle, and shared the favours of Mrs Armistead. They had laughed or stormed together about his deplorable father, the King. Had he not put all his personal weight behind Charles so few months ago and, in partnership with the flamboyant Duchess of Devonshire, carried him to victory in the Westminster election when the Parliamentary seats of so many other liberal Whigs had been lost to Pitt's grim Tories? Had he not thrown open the gardens of Carlton House to celebrate that victory, providing such music and entertainment that the jubilation was heard all along the Mall to Buckingham House? And this was his reward: Fox's broad, amiable, self-indulgent face no longer amiable and indulgent but stern.

'I love Mrs Fitzherbert.'

'There are other species of connection.'

'I have promised her marriage.'

'Then by virtue of the Royal Marriage Act,' said Fox into his wine-glass, 'you'll forfeit the Crown.'

'That damned nonsense — '

'Devised by His Majesty for just such a princely whim.'

'Whim? There'll never be another but Maria. I swear it.'

'To be sure.' Fox forced a smile. 'But any marriage contracted by you before your twenty-fifth birthday without the King's consent will be declared invalid. Furthermore, it's a condition of the Act of Settlement that the throne will be denied you if you take a Catholic for wife.'

'Maria and I shall be married whether the King likes it or not, whether you like it or not — '

'And whether Mrs Fitzherbert likes it or not?' said Fox dryly.

'I cannot endure to live without her as wife. She must come back.'

'And if she will not?'

'Then I . . . dammit it, then I shall go to her.'

He had vowed that to her, and now he would make it come true. Fox's protests died away; or else perhaps they were ceasing to be audible through the phrases George was already rehearsing in his mind. He would go to see his father at once. His father demanded that he should economize. Very well, he knew how that might be achieved. Now, surely, he and his father would see eye to eye? It was all so simple.

He sent for his carriage and set out for Windsor.

The King received him with marked lack of cordiality. Suspicion lurked in the dour corners of his always pouting mouth, and there was a twitch in his right eye which the Prince had observed two or three times in recent encounters. Was it simply a tic of bad temper, or was there something physically wrong with his father? There had been whispers of occasional fits of rage turning to deep depression, of rambling soliloquies which grew more and more hysterical. But the Queen protected her husband from all save his most trusted servitors, and one could glean little of the truth.

At this moment George was prepared to be patient with his father's real or imagined illnesses. He had to be.

'Majesty, I have had a splendid idea.'

'Surrounded by Ionic colonnades and floored in marble, no doubt.'

'Papa, please bear with me. I have been conscious of your concern for my welfare, and now I believe I can see a way of meeting your strictest demands. I have decided it would be good for me to settle abroad, at least for a few years. To broaden my education, to keep away from contentious elements in this country, and to practise a system of the strictest economy.'

He waited for the dawn of approval.

King George began to pace jerkily up and down the drawing-room. Once he stopped and glared out of the window as if debating whether or not to summon his bodyguard, then resumed his progress. Words jerked out of him to the rhythm of his footsteps.

'Strictest economy? Nonsense. Why not start here, eh, what-what?'

'Here I am too well known.'

'And you'd make yourself even more conspicuous abroad. Never heard of a project so replete with mischief. Fifty thousand pounds a year from me, and the Duchy of Cornwall gives you another thirteen thousand. Yet your debts mount to the skies, whilst your sole visible concern remains the pursuit of a life of idleness.'

George forced himself to keep his voice steady. 'I have pointed out before, Majesty, that I did not choose that life of idleness. It was chosen for me by you.'

'What-what? Mm?' The King's eyes swivelled alarmingly, and stared at something far off towards infinity. 'And how do you propose,' he cried at random, 'to repay the Treasury your debt of one hundred and sixty thousand pounds? One hundred and — '

'Not by staying in England, Majesty,' said his son earnestly. 'To achieve retrenchments I must become anonymous. I shall be no disgrace to you, I vow it. I shall live abroad in unostentatious retirement.'

'Retirement? Abroad? Are you unaware that the successor to the Crown can never quit the realm without permission of the Sovereign?'

'Evidently I'm aware of it, or I should not be here. I am here, Papa, proposing that I should lead a simple life, that you should simply give permission — '

'Simply nothing. There will be no more talk of your travelling abroad, let alone settling there.'

'I will prove to you, Papa, that — '

'You will remain in this country.' The King had halted with his plumply bowed legs apart and those disturbingly popping eyes staring an undisguised detestation. 'And you will eschew all further profligacy and extravagance. If you wish to bask in good opinions, then strive to regain the good opinion of this nation; since once lost it can never be regained.' He took a deep, shuddering breath. 'You are dismissed, sir.'

The Prince felt his own knees shudder with rage. He was near to collapse but would not demean himself before this monster. He bowed and turned, and was stalking from the room when there came a final screech from his father:

'Once lost it can *never be regained*!'

The Prince glanced back. But the King appeared to be addressing the wall, his face collapsing like a crumpled mask. George hesitated; but it had been made clear that civilized discussion was impossible between them, and he hurried on.

Since he was not allowed, however discreetly, to pursue Maria, he must renew his efforts to bring her back.

He wrote an impassioned letter. A special courier was despatched with instructions not to return until Mrs Fitzherbert had been tracked down. The task was not too difficult. By the time confirmation came, George had already penned another letter some twenty pages long; and then another, even longer.

Debilitated by the after-effects of his wound, cut deeper than he had perhaps quite intended, and by that demoralizing clash with his father, he no longer had the strength to cope with late-night revelry at Brooks's Club, nor the appetite for those ladies of the Court or elsewhere who showed such willingness to divert him. He wanted no tawdry diversions; yet must recuperate, must somehow fill in the gaps between his intensive bouts of letter-writing.

Folk were speaking well of Brighton, the increasingly fashionable Sussex watering-place. Sea air was good for one, sea bathing even better. He would take a cottage there, walk and meditate, possibly seek health in the salt water. And always by his side would walk, in spirit, Maria.

Brighton was all it had been declared to be. The rented cottage was small but charming. If he could buy a more commodious property here and get the admirable Holland to adapt it to his needs, what better place could there be for an unobtrusive married life, near to his beloved and far from his father's derogatory eye?

Strolling along the Steine towards the glittering water into which brawny 'dippers' lowered ladies venturing with many a squeal and giggle from their bathing chariots, he yearned for Maria to be on his arm, brushing her cheek against his, offering her sweet breath and sweet skin where he could taste and touch.

From the cottage he sent out his weary courier with more letters. His pleas followed Maria Fitzherbert from Paris to Aix-la-Chapelle, on to the Hague, and off through the Alps. He offered her a true marriage: not merely the symbolic one which that first ring might have seemed to suggest, but a true and lasting marriage.

Damn his father, damn the Royal Marriage Act, damn the Act of Settlement. Maria should come home. If the King thundered, the Prince would follow his impulse to abandon all he possessed in England and do what many subjects of the Crown were doing with increased enthusiasm: he and his bride would seek happiness in the newly free, welcoming land of America. That, of all things, would be a rightful retribution on his father.

First, though, Maria must be brought where he could speak to her face to face and win her over.

He called on her friend and Fox's ally, the Duchess of Devonshire, to write and intercede on his behalf; and paid no heed to Fox's reiterated warnings. When there was no response, his letters grew ever more fervent. Surely no woman of such sweet sensibility as Mrs Fitzherbert could resist such heartbreaking entreaties?

Even so, he was incredulous when his harassed courier finally brought the news. Mrs Fitzherbert was on her way back to London and would be honoured to receive him in Park Street on her return.

It could mean only one thing.

The watchful Fox knew what was afoot but did not know how far it would go. His warnings grew more severe until he burst out unhappily in a letter as impassioned, in its own way, as some of the Prince's.

> The sum of my humble advice, nay, of my most earnest entreaty, is this – that your Royal Highness would not think of marrying until you can marry legally . . . In the meantime, a mock Marriage (for it can be no other) is neither honourable for any of the parties nor, with respect to your Royal Highness, even safe. This appears so clear to me that if I were Mrs Fitzherbert's father or brother I would advise her not by any means to agree to

it, and to prefer any species of connection with you to one leading to so much misery and mischief.

Was Charles worried for his own political future? It had always been implicit that when at last the Prince of Wales became King, it would mean swift promotion for Fox and Sheridan to high posts in the land. They would stand little chance of such elevation if their names were involved with that of an illegal and irreligious scandal.

But no. The Prince would not interpret the warning in such a light. Whatever his own ambitions, Charles was first and foremost a friend and had taken the liberty of writing in this manner only because of that friendship. With tears in his eyes, George wrote to reassure him.

Make yourself easy, my dear friend. Believe me, the world will now soon be convinced that there not only is, but never was, any grounds for these reports, which of late have been so malevolently circulated.

He wrote this in the small hours of a Sunday morning in December 1785. On the Thursday afternoon of that same week he and Maria Fitzherbert were wed in the privacy of her Park Street house. The Prince had found an Anglican clergyman willing to perform the ceremony: the Reverend John Burt, newly released from a debtor's prison on the discharge of his £500 liability. The bride found two witnesses: her brother Jack and her uncle Henry Errington, both Catholics and both unsure of the wisdom of these proceedings, but fond enough of Maria to fall in with her wishes.

'If any man can show any cause why they may not lawfully be joined together, let him now speak, or else hereafter for ever hold his peace.'

Thank heavens that Fox was not here to raise a voice; or the King; or any of the royal household likely ever to speak of this unseemly matter. Sweat trickled from the Prince's brow at the mere thought.

As Burt droned to a conclusion, and Maria's hand with the ring upon it was in her husband's, she said in an undertone: 'Do you regret this, my dear?'

'I love you.'

'You're perspiring. I thought perhaps — '

'I was delayed on the way here, and dared not seem in too great a hurry.'

'Delayed by some lady to whom you were bidding farewell?'

'My dear, my love — '

'Or Mr Fox, persuading you against me?'

'No, no.'

The Prince looked gratefully round as the two witnesses came forward to kiss Maria and shake him deferentially by the hand. 'We shall live happy ever after,' he said loudly, and laughed, and Maria was smiling and close to him and he knew his campaign of conquest had been a worthy one and the rewards would be exquisite.

The dark of winter afternoon had settled over the city when they left in Maria's coach for the briefest of honeymoons at a secluded lodge in Surrey.

'You have told Mr Fox of this marriage?' Maria returned to the subject as they clattered away down the street, sitting well back from the guttering of an occasional lantern or the brighter glow of spacious windows.

'I . . . er . . . I confess I hedged a little. Confide in him when the moment's right, you know. Have to be discreet.'

Dubiously she edged away from him, but before she could frame a question he dragged her back, turned her face to his and held her tight. For a second she resisted, then was laughing again: not, this time, in that slightly remote, condescending way, but with a laugh of unaffected joy.

They kissed. When their lips reluctantly separated and a faint hazy light brushed across her forehead, Maria said:

'My dearest, it is for you to declare that we are man and

wife. Never in your lifetime will I admit to being your wife until you say it is right to do so.'

'But you *are* my wife.'

'The fact that it's true is enough.'

They were locked in each other's arms again for an eternity, lost, ecstatic.

Suddenly the coach lurched and tilted slowly, dizzily sideways so that the bride collapsed in a huddle across her bridegroom's knees. A door flew open, and the Prince had to brace one foot against the jamb in order not to fall out and take Maria with him.

'What the devil . . .?'

The coachman staggered round, squelching in a wide swathe of mud.

'Your Royal Highness, I'm most profoundly sorry.'

'Should think so. Dammit, what's happened?'

'A wheel has come off, your Royal — '

'What?' Cautiously George leaned out, trying to conjure some recognizable feature from the darkness. 'A wilderness! Where in heaven's name are we?'

'A place called Hammersmith, sir.'

Maria let out a sad little moan.

George hastened to reassure her. 'Even in Hammersmith dearest of wives, there's bound to be an inn to welcome impatient lovers.'

Her weight was upon him, and he loved it to be so. Close to his ear she began to chuckle. It was an infuriating accident at such a time, on such a night; yet funny, something they would look back on when they were old and still happy together.

This would yet be the sweetest night of their lives.

CHAPTER FOUR

The Prince of Wales lay in bed. Daylight streamed in through the pale yellow curtains, which seemed to dance a slow sarabande to the gently swaying shadows of elm trees in Carlton House garden. He heaved himself up against huge, plumped-up pillows, and browsed through the paragraphs of the London Gazette.

> We are informed that the lovely Mrs F. has attended Drury Lane Theatre for a performance of Mr Sheridan's operetta *The Duenna.* She was attended to her box by a certain person . . .

George pushed himself up on one elbow. ' "By a certain person",' he quoted aloud, ' "but it was observed that she was not permitted to hang her arm upon him." Not permitted! It reads as though I drove you off with a cudgel.' He stared indignantly over the edge of the paper at Maria, seated at her dressing-table and examining her face dreamily in the glass: his wife, really his wife, hard as it still was to believe. She shook a tumult of hair back over her shoulders into the bright wintry sunlight, and blew a kiss to him in the mirror. 'Most adorable one, come back to bed.'

'All play and no work,' she said in that husky tone he had come to cherish, 'transforms George into a greasy fat dumpling.'

'You think I'm a clown. One of my father's red-nosed favourites. Not that *I've* ever been one of his favourites.'

She rose from her dressing-table and came to sit on the bed, but evaded his hand as he reached for the softness of her thigh.

'I did once think of you as a jester,' she said. 'But now I know better what is at the heart of your being.'

When their eyes met, to George it was as immediate as if their flesh were touching again, as if his hands were exploring her again and being lovingly coaxed along and then teased, tapped aside only to be accepted again with passion all the greater for the delay.

'Tell me,' he urged.

'It would make you conceited. You would begin to wonder why you had thrown yourself away on me.'

'Never say that, never again. Never think it, Maria.'

Through her he was fulfilled. Did she not see the difference she had made? Through her he had found himself. He asked so little now – yet it was so much.

As if she saw his intentions in his eyes and was anxious not to be snared again, she jumped up. 'A pity that you are still such a lie-a-bed, though. It's a quarter past ten o'clock, George, and we're to meet Mr Holland at noon.'

'Mr Holland is used to my unpunctuality.'

'Today you will be on time for Mr Holland. Here.' She snatched up a handful of fashion plates from her dressing-table and threw them on to his folded London Gazette. 'Tell me what I am to wear.'

In a sweeter, more loving world she should wear nothing; should ride naked through the streets to the wonder of all who beheld her. But this present world demanded other standards. George turned over a coloured print of a stiffly buttoned bodice and skirt, then a loose drapery in pink and blue with a high lacy ruff. Slyly he peeped at Maria, letting a wisp of silk fall from her warm shoulder.

He said: 'I like the sprigged muslin.'

She glanced at the plate. 'It is georgette. And if I wore such a pattern, would you be able to distinguish me from the wallpaper?'

'It's not the least like wallpaper.'

'It is. But very nice wallpaper.'

He lay back in the comfort of his cushions and watched her at her toilet. He was the happiest man in the world. This was contentment, and should remain so. When the moment was right he would declare himself, and reign over his people as a bachelor monarch with a wife at his side though she could never be queen. Because of that they would be freed from the care of carrying on the dynasty: in due course the crown could pass to his brother Frederick's children – when he managed some legitimate ones – and everyone would live happily ever after.

Already his Maria was accompanying him everywhere. The London Gazette and the Brighton newspapers and the gossips of town and city knew that one could not be invited without the other. At receptions in Carlton House, Mrs Fitzherbert implicitly took precedence over the duchesses and countesses who came to marvel at the exotic splendours of the garden or the Gothic conservatory. At her own assemblies she was soon accepted as the most accomplished hostess in the capital – and one who could always guarantee royalty among her guests. Their nights they spent sometimes in that sumptuous bedroom above the Mall, sometimes in her house in Park Street. If he had been out roistering with his friends she would wait up to make sure he came safely home, and hide from their drunken blunderings in mock terror until he had prised her out from behind a sofa or screen. At Brighton they rose late, went riding together, went to the races together, walked arm in arm along the promenade; and she had her own decorous little house no more than a few minutes' stroll from the Prince's farmhouse which Holland was converting into a little marine pavilion.

George had further plans for the pavilion. If his debts could be cleared, or if he could find some other source of loans, one day he would embark on a more ambitious building programme. But for the time being the two of them were happy with things as they were. If Maria was wary of Fox and Sheridan when they came to dine or revel, and avoided Fox's keenly challenging gaze as if afraid that her very expression would answer the question that continued to fret him, and if the public prints and cartoonists all too often came out with bolder and bolder suggestions along similar lines, these were no more than questions and suggestions. George went out of his way to reassure his old friend – though not in Maria's presence. Marriage? If such a thing could not legally be – as Charles himself had made plain it could not be – then how could it be at all? The jibes of the journals were best answered by ignoring them. Within the ornate walls of Carlton House or the snug seclusion of the Brighton farmhouse, the lovers were at ease; and forever loving.

It could not last. Within a year of their secret marriage the King, perhaps made uneasy by tales of an avaricious widow battening on his son, was once more asking for an account of that son's debts. There were the same recriminations, the same demands for retrenchment. But this time George had a wife to lean on and to advise him. He did not care for some of her recommendations; but the promises that went with them softened his resistance.

To the King's surprise, the Prince of Wales closed Carlton House, dismissed a large number of his servants, sold his racing stud and most of his carriages, and went off to lead a simple life at the seaside – taking with him the woman whose presence would alleviate some of that simplicity.

In Brighton, vowed the Prince, they would live an idyll of modest plenty, feeding on love.

Colonel Hotham, the Treasurer appointed by his father, had to admit on a visit that he was favourably impressed.

'It looks good in the accounts, does it not?' said the Prince affably. 'Sober and industrious. Well, maybe not industrious. But sober certainly. I buy my claret by the dozen bottles these days, so stocks are permanently low – especially if Sheridan has been visiting, as he is now.'

'You find life irksome, your Royal Highness?'

'Quite the contrary. It has been a revelation to me, this modest life at Brighton. This is how we should live, Hotham, all of us. All I lack is work – some responsibility which I *ought* to have, some way of contributing to the welfare of my country.' It was not a subject on which he had dwelt much of late, but a few of Maria's remarks and now the presence of Hotham stirred old ideas and old resentments. 'Have you seen His Majesty of late?'

'I had that honour three days ago. His Majesty,' said Hotham placatingly, 'was most suitably impressed by your quarterly accounts which I showed him. He is now more favourably inclined towards you, sir, than he has been for a long time.'

'Frugality being, as ever, equivalent in his mind to virtue.' George tugged irritably at a plated button on his olive-green riding coat. The buttons should have been on a uniform. 'Favourably disposed, you say? Favourably enough to grant me some of my rights as heir to the throne? To let me play a part in the defence of the country, and to grant me more than a wretched pittance to go with it?'

'I . . . perhaps it is too soon to hope for that, your Royal Highness.'

Hotham's embarrassment was overridden by the sudden eruption of Richard Sheridan, reeling into the room as if but newly disembarked from a stormy Channel crossing.

'I have taken your advice, my friend' – he steadied himself with an arm about the Prince's shoulders – 'and stood in the gardens and breathed the brine in the air.'

'And now you know, Sherry — '

'Now I know that I'm a Londoner. My eyes are scorched by the salt, there's a buzzing in my ears, and my hands . . . look . . .' He extended one hand, shaking within its stained yellow cuff, became aware of Hotham for the first time, and twitched fingers even more shakily in the Colonel's direction. 'Colonel Hotham, how are you?'

'Well, Mr Sheridan, well.'

'Then leave here immediately. This is no place for healthy people.'

'I'm healthier than ever before,' the Prince pointed out, 'and I remain.'

Sheridan straightened up. His long oval face seemed to lengthen, until his chin dipped into the puffed-out folds of his cravat. The cynical lines drooping from the corners of his mouth deepened. 'You remain because you must. You're a prisoner, your Royal Highness. But your friends in London have not forgotten the fugitive. We talk of dear dead days, and talk and talk again. I shall not flatter you by repeating what we say.'

George thought of Carlton House, shuttered and silent. Of the rumbustious nights in cheerfully low company, and of the high Whig ideals to which he had once given his support. Then there had been a Prince's party. And now – now they missed him? There were new clashes in Parliament, he heard of them quickly enough in Brighton, and Sherry was here to verify them. Ought he not to be back in London beside his friends, showing them that he had not deserted?

That night after dinner, when Sheridan and two other guests had retired early before their legs betrayed them, George and his Maria strolled in the gardens.

She came out with it at once. 'I wish they hadn't come.'

'You'd keep me from my friends?'

'Indeed I would not. And yet I don't think they are good friends. Not your Mr Sheridan.'

'He amuses me.' George remembered a brilliant ten minutes of Richard's inspired buffoonery at table: the sparkle and wit and inventiveness which made his plays such a success and his political speeches so devastating.

'Yes, he's the court jester. But a cunning one, and a dangerous one. He wants power.'

'We all do, in one way and another. *I* want power.'

'And whenever Mr Sheridan appears in our company, he reminds you of it. Are you not content here?'

'Of course I'm content.' The Prince spoke a trifle too defiantly. 'I assure you I'm content. Living a delightful dream. But one must be prepared for reality sometimes. My father shows signs of being well-disposed towards me at last. If I were to press for an increase in my Civil List payments and eradication of my debts, and we returned to London — '

'To London?' cried Maria, dismayed.

'London and Brighton, we'll have both.' The one, he thought blissfully, to strike against the other, to set each other off, city and country, artifice and nature. What more delightful balance? 'In London,' he declared, 'with my status assured financially I'll be able to . . . why, I swear I shall . . .'

'Destroy yourself.'

He disengaged his arm from hers. They still walked side by side but there was a long silence until he said:

'You have no faith in me.'

'George, listen to me,' she said gently, seeking his arm again. 'One day you will be a great king. You have the seeds of it within you, but your talent needs husbanding. Until your father's death – I must say this to you, my love – you will receive nothing but the flattery of your associates and the insults of your enemies. And neither one will help you achieve the necessary dignity for your future.'

It grew more hurtful. 'I have no dignity?'

'I mean in the eyes of the people. They have been fed too many lies about you, George, not to be suspicious.'

'I will talk to Fox.'

'Ah, yes. Mr Fox also is out for power.'

'He is my friend. And the greatest man in England.'

'A great man,' she conceded: 'a champion of liberty, an idealist. But he needs power if those ideals are ever to come to fruition. He needs *you* . . . until you are in a position to grant him that power. Then he may need you no longer. If only you were more popular among the people!'

The Prince bowed his head. Through lies, through

scandal-mongering and malice and misinterpretation, through the vicious tricks of the print-makers and the blatant antagonism of his father, he was popular with no one. Those who did not know him had been given a convenient ogre to hate.

'Fox' – he groped for something to cling to – 'will never use me false. He'll never betray me.'

He must call his true friends down here for a serious talk. Or return to them.

Before he could make a decision, it was made for him. Henry Holland wished the farmhouse empty so that he could start work on the central classical rotunda and complete the transition into his planned marine pavilion.

Back to London, then. If there was to be a fray, the Prince of Wales ought to be in it.

CHAPTER FIVE

The cartoon was a gross caricature, and the depiction of a blowzy Mrs Fitzherbert as 'The Royal Toast: fair, fat and forty' was a gross injustice to an ample but graceful woman not yet in her thirties. Nevertheless Charles James Fox allowed himself a small, sour smile. Mrs Fitzherbert was no toast of his. Her influence on the Prince had been detrimental to that of the Prince's friends. And in whatever light some other place-seekers might see George, Fox still saw him as a friend. Wayward, unpredictable, but a friend – and one who must return to them.

So he did not entirely disapprove of Gillray's savaging of Mrs Fitz.

He was less amused when a fresh libel appeared. In this, with the caption ' 'Twas Nobody saw the Lovers Leap', he found himself sketched in the rôle of Nobody, urging the Prince of Wales to leap into matrimony with an even more grossly travestied Mrs Fitzherbert.

In the lobby of the Palace of Westminster they laughed heartily enough. That is, most of them laughed. John Rolle, the aggressive Member for North Devon, was waving the print about but ranting rather than laughing. And Fox could not summon up even a smile as he approached and had the picture brandished under his nose.

'And here comes Mr Nobody himself, my friends.' The rich Devonian burr rasped up and back from the echoing ceiling. 'That very same Mr Nobody who's privy to certain plottings of the Vicar of Rome.'

In the shocked hush Fox turned to Sheridan at his elbow. 'The Vicar of Rome? Richard, pray enlighten me. To whom does the Honourable Member refer?'

'I really can't conceive. For myself,' said Sheridan with

a yawn, 'I take the greatest care never to travel further south than Brighton.'

'You take my meaning, Mr Sheridan, you take it very well,' growled Rolle. 'And you, Mr Nobody-Fox: tell us, do there be or do there not be a conspiracy between yourself and that same Vicar of Rome to elevate a Catholic whore and crown her Queen of England?'

'Mr Rolle, I'm as good and loyal a Protestant as the next man. I have never met the Pope in Rome or had any communication with him.'

'But tell us this, then: be they or bain't they man and wife?'

'I assure you, Mr Rolle,' said Fox as patiently as he could manage, 'that this is nothing but another of His Royal Highness's passing fancies.'

Rolle stabbed a forefinger at the cartoon. 'The Prince has had many a passing fancy, but never none like this.' He turned contemptuously away. 'There be no smoke without fire.'

Fox and Sheridan waited for other Members to disperse. Then Fox swore. 'Damn the man. Damn him.'

'He could prove tedious, could he not?'

'Not Rolle. The Prince. Damn the Prince of Wales, and damn that woman of his.'

But when George and his Maria returned to London, and Fox and Sheridan were summoned to Carlton House, they went speedily. It was imperative to reclaim the Prince.

Already they knew that old pride was rekindling in that swelling, pouter-pigeon breast. The Duc d'Orléans had been approached and had allowed himself to hint that money might be raised for the Prince in France. And well it might, thought Fox apprehensively. Usurers in troubled France were looking for safe havens abroad. But if the Prince were to be restrained from such dabblings, it would only be in the hope of Parliament providing for him.

'We can't support him,' said Fox as they waited for their audience.

'We need him, Charles.'

'We don't need a man living openly with a Roman Catholic mistress. A liaison with which I'm supposed to sympathize – supposed to have encouraged! *I*!' Moving away from the two footmen stationed at the inner doors, Fox lowered his voice. 'He should have tired of her by now. All this time closeted with that mimsy madam – how has he tolerated it?'

'From my observation,' murmured Sheridan, 'a few more months penned together in that farmhouse would have broken them apart. Boredom would have done it.'

'Then we must get him back there and keep him there. Pen him up in Brighton, destroy that woman's hold over him, and . . .'

He stopped as the doors were flung open and the Prince entered with arms outstretched.

'Charles, my dear Charles! It gives me strength just to look at you.'

'Your Royal Highness —'

'George, dammit, I'm called George.'

'George.'

'Better, oh, so much better. Now.' The Prince waved them both to chairs, but instead of being seated himself began to stamp in a wavering circle around them. 'There are things we must decide. Charles, for a start I must have money.'

'George —'

'My debts must be paid, Charles, and my income increased. Parliament must vote it. Not an unreasonable request, is it? Haven't I proved my worth, shown how diligently I can economize? My Maria has nothing and asks for nothing: not a penny spent on jewellery, and there are neither wines in my cellars nor paintings on my walls. I'm a reformed character. I need this to be acknowledged. Charles, I need your oratory.'

He came to a halt in front of his old friend. Fox could not repress a smile of warm complicity. The young man was so impossible, so impetuous, so absurd – and so irresistibly endearing. It was well-nigh impossible to keep a cool head in his presence. But it had to be done.

Carefully he said: 'George, Protestant feeling in the country is running high. There are rumours, the print shops are playing on them and selling out.'

'Selling trash.'

'Indeed, yes. But they create a feeling that we, the English, are under siege. The national character is threatened.'

'Such a feeling is certainly not apparent in Brighton.'

'It is forcibly apparent in London. It stems . . .' He took a deep breath, and stabbed the words out as harshly as possible. 'It stems from the now long-standing liaison between the heir to the throne and a Roman Catholic woman.'

'Have a care, Charles. Maria is my . . . my love, the only profound love I have ever possessed. And so she will remain.'

'Then I have to tell you that to support in Parliament your request for further monies would mean the destruction of all your friends in the Whig party.'

'You can't mean it.'

'We would be seen as envoys of Rome. Catholicism is a strain, George, which too easily contaminates.'

'Does it, by heaven?' The Prince's voice cracked in petulant protest. 'Then this country is filled with fools, and I'll have no more of them. I renounce my position here and now. I renounce my title to the throne. My brother Frederick shall be king.'

'If you do this — '

'I'll do it, sir. I'll write a deed now. You shall have it and I shall have no more degrading tomfoolery.'

'Then there will be other consequences,' said Fox. 'Your income will not be increased but reduced to fit your new status. Just another Hanoverian princeling. In affect, a self-elected commoner. Your little Brighton pavilion will perforce become your first and only residence.'

'This is infamous!' Turning from Fox's stern gaze to

Sheridan, the Prince implored: 'Richard, what am I to do?'

Sheridan did not risk exchanging a glance with his colleague, but said: 'If you will only wait a little longer – return to Brighton for a few months more, let us be judges of the time to approach Parliament. Then perhaps all will not be lost.'

'And if I do not wish to?'

'We cannot support you at this moment.'

Sheridan left alone. The Prince slumped into a chair. Then his disconsolate face began to brighten. Hopefully he glanced at Fox, still here with him. 'Charles, you've got something else to suggest?'

'Something to ask, rather. A question which must be answered.'

The cheerfulness faded. The Prince was ready to relapse into sulkiness.

Fox said implacably: 'Did you or did you not go through a form of marriage with Mrs Fitzherbert?'

'Oh, that.' George tried to wave it bluffly away. 'The question's irrelevant, Charles. You've thrust the Royal Marriage Act at me from your own lips. No such ceremony would have any force in law.'

'Legality or lack of it is not the point. Such a union would have *political* force. Of the wrong kind. The Tories would be provided with ammunition to destroy us. It's bad enough that you should live with her. But the Protestant succession in the hands of a Catholic . . . and a Catholic commoner, without even a diplomatic dowry! George, I beg you: assure me that the story of this reputed ceremony is untrue.'

The Prince's fingers plucked at ruffled lace, at the tight nankin about his haunches, and at his own fingers until they were interlaced in impromptu prayer.

'I love her, Charles. She would not have me, she rejected me – or, rather, that accursed religion of hers forced her to. What could I do, Charles, what could I do?'

'You *have* married her,' said Fox in despair.

'No, no, it's not so,' said George hastily. 'I've had to . . . well . . . make promises. I admit I've made promises. In the future, when it's safe, I might . . . that is, I've promised I will . . . regularize our relationship. But she understands. Truly, Charles, she does understand. And on those terms she accepted me.'

The warmth of bewildered affection suffused Fox's heart and mind again. How typical of the man: naïve, romantic, clumsy and yet, with his woman as with his friends, ultimately getting his way. Who else would have played such a devious game? The situation was not good, thought Fox; but it might have been worse. He rose to go.

With the sly eagerness of a child seeking a reward for exemplary behaviour, the Prince said: 'And as to those funds of which we spoke, Charles?'

'We've told you, nothing can be done yet awhile.'

'Not directly, no. But might there not be some other Member who'd not involve you personally but could still speak on behalf of the heir to the throne and what's due to him?'

'Patience is your only support,' said Fox. 'For your own sake I suggest you go to Windsor and set the King's mind at rest by telling him what you've told me, so he may discount aught else he hears. Then patience, and more patience.'

As he strolled up towards Brooks's his own earnest injunction set up a mocking echo in his head. Patience, indeed: when had George, Prince of Wales, ever practised such a virtue?

But surely the man had no choice now. The position had been made brutally plain. There was no one else to speak up on his behalf.

It came as a shock when Alderman Newnham, a very solemn City merchant who had methodically paid his way into the House but not thereafter paid enough to warrant any significant promotion, stood up to propound the terms of a motion 'That a humble address be presented to His

Majesty praying him to take into consideration the present embarrassed state of the finances of the Prince of Wales, and to grant him an appropriate measure of financial relief, to be made good by this House.'

A groundswell of surprise was spattered with grunts of disapproval. Fox glanced along the bench at Sheridan, whose consternation obviously equalled his own. Who had put the egregious Newnham up to this? What promises of future preferment – Fox's heart sank – had the manouevring Prince made to this nonentity? Nothing else could explain such a motion at such a time.

Rolle was on his feet. 'Mr Speaker, before this Honourable House goes on to debate the motion now proposed, I must ask – nay, I will demand, for the good repute of this House – from Mr Pitt and his administration assurances of a delicate nature which go immediately to affect our constitution in church and state. If we are to consider further payments to His Royal Highness we must needs be acquainted with the truths underlying certain rumours.'

Fox groaned. He could almost exonerate the Prince and believe that the instigator was the cantankerous Rolle, putting Newnham up to it simply in order to have a chance of insinuating his question.

Pitt was answering. 'My administration is most keenly aware of the point raised by the Member for North Devon. I wish most profoundly that I were able to give the assurances he seeks, but I have to admit these are circumstances in which I am not privy to the truth.' His lean, predatory head swung towards the bench where Fox and Sheridan sat. 'It could be that certain members of the Opposition are better placed to reassure the Honourable Member.'

'Come on, old Fox-face.' Rolle was rubicund and greeful. 'A-huntin' we will go, a-huntin' we will go, we'll catch a fox and . . .'

The rising babble of outraged invective drowned him him out. Newnham was trying to make himself heard, but

Rolle shouted him down and bellowed more forcefully through the uproar.

'Come on, Foxy-face, give us thy story. Be they married or bain't they?'

There was no evading it. Fox rose to his feet and waited until the hubbub had died down.

'Mr Speaker, sir. These insinuations thrown out against His Royal Highness, from whatever quarter they may have come, are in the extreme illiberal, unjust and rancorous.'

'Get to the main point,' grated the venomous Devonian voice. 'Is he married to the Catholic whore?'

'In this House, Mr Speaker, where it is known how frequently the falsehoods of the time are circulated, I would have hoped that a tale fit only to impose on the lowest — '

'Aye,' Rolle insisted. 'And there's the Royal Dukes. They receive her, do they not, and are received by her?'

'When such calumny has been circulated with such industry.' Fox persevered, 'it proves at once the uncommon pains taken by His Royal Highness's enemies.'

'Be they or bain't they man and wife? True or nay?'

Into the tremulous silence Fox said: 'Not true.' He thought of George's ludicrous evasions and of the lies his friend must have fed that troublesome woman. 'The matter could never have happened legally,' he said with a conviction which reducing any lingering sneer to mute respect. 'And never did happen in any way whatsoever. It has been from the beginning a base and malicious falsehood. Let that be an end to the matter. As for the motion put before us this day, I hereby append my humble but wholehearted support.'

Cheers and jumbled protests swamped anything else he might have wished to add. But there was nothing really to add. The Prince of Wales was a feckless fool; but surely not feckless enough to marry a Catholic, and not fool enough to deceive his most reliable friend. If that were ever shown to be untrue, then all so-called truth was itself a shabby mockery.

CHAPTER SIX

Clouds which had smeared the blue morning sky were beginning to darken that blue, and a greying heaviness lay upon Brighton. The green of the garden below the Prince's window had been robbed of its lustre.

So had Maria's usually high colour, now mottled with anger. She flung into the room and tossed a copy of the London Advertiser on a chair near the Prince.

It was no use waiting for her accusation. He had to take the plunge. 'You've read the reports of Fox's speech?'

'Which I take to be accurate?' she said icily.

'Oh, are such things ever accurate?'

'He did deny our marriage.'

'It seems . . . well, yes, he did.'

'So it comes to this. In the greatest debating chamber in the world, a leading statesman, great orator, friend of princes, has publicly stigmatized me as a common strumpet.'

'You're too harsh. I'm sure Charles was doing his best to — '

'A kept woman.'

'Dearest Maria.' George spread his arms wide so that she might rush into them. She walked past him and stared unseeingly out of the window. 'You yourself warned me that Fox is a political creature,' he pleaded. 'Clearly he felt an open assertion of the true facts would be unwise. He could be right, from his point of view.'

'I'm not a fool, George.'

'Nor is Charles.'

'No. No, he is not. Fox would not deliberately have lied, not on a matter of this moment. A lie to the Commons? No, your Mr Fox believed he was telling nothing but the truth. Now why should he believe that?' When he did not reply she turned upon him. 'I never thought you could cause me so much pain.'

'You're not accusing me of telling Fox that — '

'Do you deny it?'

'Of course I deny it.'

'Then I don't believe you.' She seemed about to strike him; but then put her chin proudly back. 'I've given up so much for you, George. In return I am given what? A hole-and-corner marriage to a husband I can no longer trust. This act of yours has shown that you . . . that you have a crippled heart.'

'I don't understand you, Maria.' Could she not see the tears in his eyes and feel his suffering? 'There's been a speech, yes, an unfortunate speech if you like. But it'll be forgotten. It doesn't signify. We are man and wife, whatever may be said in public.'

She was staring at him in wonder. 'You still don't comprehend me. Can you not know what you've done? *You* instigated this vile business. *You* misled Fox, knowing as you did so that the only possible outcome would be that your dearest and most loving wife would be publicly traduced, branded a whore, betrayed and humiliated. I have kept silent, as I promised I would. But you – what have *you* done? And for what reason? For money. Money! You knew what would happen and you didn't mind, it didn't matter that my name, honour, position would be besmirched by your greed. I'm leaving you, George.'

'You couldn't. Maria, I know how it seems in the heat of the moment, but — '

'I can no longer bear to be with you.' A sob was dragged from her. 'But be of good heart, George. The lie won't stick now, because I shan't be here to give it any substance. I'm returning to London.'

'Maria, we'll go together, I'll show the world — '

'I shall not receive you again.'

She drew up her skirts in a rustle of defiance and swept from the room.

Fox paused on the step of Brooks's and surveyed the clattering, congested traffic of St James's. He began to think of skittish phrases with which to attack that young upstart Pitt in the House tomorrow. There were so many vantage points from which he might launch his barbs.

A gentleman coming into the club stopped and turned towards him. 'Mr Fox.'

'Sir?'

'My name is Errington. Henry Errington.'

'A pleasure to make your acquaintance, sir.'

'I am the uncle of Mrs Fitzherbert.'

Fox felt an inexplicable chill. He trusted the fellow was not going to make an indignant scene within these respectable portals. 'Indeed, sir?'

'I hear that you have denied in the House of Commons her marriage to the Prince of Wales.'

'With good reason, sir.'

'With very poor reason, sir. You have been misinformed. I was myself present at the wedding. My nephew was another witness. There were also two servants in attendance. It is not a story which can be denied long, sir. As one who has hitherto admired you, I fear for your political future.' Errington strode on into the club. 'Good-day, Mr Fox.'

The news from Windsor was unexpected and alarming. Or might it, in the Prince's present misery and sense of irreparable loss, prove after all a blessing if considered in the right light? There was only one way to establish what lay behind these disquieting tales. Frederick, Duke of York, was home from military service in Hanover. It was reasonable that he should go to pay his respects to his father; and reasonable that his older brother should accompany him.

They presented themselves in that Windsor antechamber where George had so often waited for a denunciation of his spendthrift habits and immorality. There could surely be no danger this time: Parliament had granted the money he required, his father had consented to make a personal addition to his income, perhaps because tales had reached him of Mrs Fitzherbert's defection, and Colonel Hotham continued to report on His Majesty's continuing amiability. Fox, embittered, was out of the country and no longer provoking the royal wrath by near-revolutionary speeches in the House. So why should there be gloom in this chamber and over the whole castle?

Fanny Burney, usually so cheerful and twinkling, came into the room and curtseyed. Her tone was as sombre as her eyes. 'The King is ready to receive your Royal Highnesses. But I must warn you, you'll find him greatly changed.'

'In what way, Miss Burney?'

'He has become . . . irascible of late. Unpredictable. I . . .' She faltered, and then stood aside so that they might precede her into the drawing-room.

King George barely raised his head to acknowledge their entry. He sat unnaturally still, hunched forward as if to stare at some spot in the carpet, with eyes darkening and glistening almost to the colour of blackcurrants. A vein stood out like an ugly knot from his temple. George and Frederick came to a dismayed halt. Their father seemed still unaware of their presence.

'Majesty,' ventured the Duke of York.

The head lifted a fraction. The eyes appeared more hideously like a dark jelly.

'Frederick.' The King's voice was feeble but he was struggling to smile. 'So you're safely returned to see me, my dear boy.'

'Safely and happily, Papa.'

'The floods did not delay you?'

'Floods, Papa?'

'You did not pass through London? London's buried by the waters. I have sent my yacht, but what can one poor vessel do in the face of the wrath of the Lord? The people are dying, Frederick, drowned, engulfed by the waters as they lie in bed, in sin, the sinks of depravity.'

The Prince felt his stomach contract, somehow wrenching over upon itself. He was sick; wanted to look away; but said shakily: 'Majesty, there are no floods in London, I assure you.'

'And when have I ever trusted to *your* assurances?' rasped his father petulantly. 'I trust Frederick. Only Frederick. But even you, my boy – I looked for you in my telescope when you were in Hanover, but could not see you. Why were you hiding?'

'Telescope, Papa?'

'A most wondrous instrument. Mr Herschel designed it to look at the moon, but I chose to look at my city of Hanover instead, and saw it most distinct – the palaces and churches, the little carts in the street. But not' – his voice thickened with anger – 'my son.' The vein stood out purple, a fleck of foam appeared at the corner of his mouth. Then he sagged forward again and was silent.

As the brothers were ushered out they found their mother, the Queen, receiving Mr Pitt. George stiffened, forcing himself reluctantly to answer the Tory leader's bow. There had never been any love lost between them.

'Mother,' Frederick was gasping, 'we must talk to you about —'

'I'll not detain you now,' said Queen Charlotte imperiously.

'But, Papa . . .'

'Mr Pitt and I have the most important business.'

On the way back to London, George and Frederick found little to say. Each was wrapped in his own thoughts, but each still saw in his mind's eye that dreadful picture. What was this affliction which had smitten their father: and why had their mother summoned Pitt to Windsor?

Explanations were not long in coming. In spite of every royal precaution against extravagant speculation, the whole of Parliament and soon the whole of London knew that the King was nigh to madness. He was foaming at the mouth in fits of rage, saw demons and terrible visions, attacked his pages and screamed at his flunkeys, yet in moments of lucidity was still apparently capable of attending to State papers and scrawling a signature where necessary. Mr Pitt was anxious to restore him to sanity. For if the King were mad but not dead, what was to be done about the constitutional procedures of the realm? Pitt knew what was proper; and knew what that would mean to his own leadership. And the Whigs knew, and the knowledge brought Sheridan hurrying to Carlton House.

'A Bill for a Regency must be prepared and passed through Parliament.'

George's pulse quickened. But his brother Frederick shook his head. 'I can't approve. Were the King to recover it would appear that — '

'The metaphor of King and Country as body and head is apt. We cannot survive without a Head of State. All administration would come to a standstill. So preparations must be made accordingly.'

'I need Fox,' said the Prince quietly.

'He's in Italy. We'll bring him back. Something like this is what he's been waiting for.'

But while Fox was on his dusty, dysentery-ridden nine-day journey home from Italy, Pitt was urging the Queen to bring in specialists in the treatment of brain disorders. 'Bedlam keepers,' she said deprecatingly; but in the face of her husband's ravings had to acquiesce.

The Reverend Thomas Willis and his brawny younger brother John were not members of the Royal College of Physicians, nor were they qualified surgeons. They had been repudiated by all orthodox medical associations – because, as they were eager to explain, of professional jealousy and the success of their unorthodox treatments. They assured their royal employer that they would break her husband's delirium by confinement and stern discipline, and then by the judicious application of hot poultices would shift the distemper from his head to his legs. They insisted, however, that there should be no visitors and no meddling criticism of their methods.

Left alone with the King, they strapped him into a strait waistcoat and then applied burning poultices to his legs. When he screamed they struck him to silence him, and tightened the straps. When he was released from his bonds and began to claw, whimpering, at his scalded legs, he was firmly imprisoned again in the waistcoat and tied to his bed. When he refused food because he could not swallow, a band was pulled across his chest and tightened.

The Prince of Wales received an exhausted Charles James Fox, but after their first excitement and exchange of grandiose plans they had to agree that as a matter of form the first discussion of a Bill of Regency must be with the Prime Minister.

Pitt accepted the need for a Regency. 'I do not, however, believe it should be unrestricted. I will present a Regency Bill to the House which, while nominating you as Regent during His Majesty's indisposition, will disbar you from making any private appointments, creating peerages, or awarding honours.'

'You wish to tie my hands completely?' protested the Prince.

'As acting Head of State you will of course have the power to dismiss my administration if it hampers you, and appoint a new one in its place.'

'You know full well that your majority means I can find no replacement for you.'

Pitt's thin-lipped smile made no pretence of hiding his distaste for the man he was forced to pay formal homage to. 'That is correct.'

'You offer me nothing, then.'

'I offer you the Regency.'

'On your terms.'

Pitt shrugged. The interview was ended. But the matter itself could not be allowed to end so. The Prime Minister's insulting terms had to be accepted for the time being. Later, if Fox could work on his allies and win others over, there might be a different Prime Minister and a different attitude. Patience: it was Fox's earlier injunction returning to plague him.

And then, just as the Bill, however unsatisfactory in particulars, was at least in train, there came the news of the King's recovery. Though much weakened by the strict Willis regimen, he was in good health and sound of mind.

The Prince of Wales and the Duke of York hurried once more to Windsor.

'Majesty.' George bowed to his father. 'This is the most joyous day of my life.'

'Dearest Papa,' said Frederick. 'I cannot express the happiness I feel to see you well.'

'Frederick, my boy.' The King's eyes were clear and lively, his voice affectionate. 'We must talk about your experiences in Hanover.'

'I long to do so, Papa.'

The King's eyes remained clear, but there was no longer any affection in them as he turned towards his eldest son. 'A Bill for a Regency?' Now his voice was cold with rage. 'You could not wait for my death, you wished to supplant me in my lifetime, what-what-what?'

'Majesty, a contingency measure was deemed necessary in case there should — '

'Silence! I see that your characteristic irresponsibility has now turned malign.'

George gasped at the injustice of it. 'It cannot have escaped Majesty's keen eye that it was Mr Pitt who deemed the Regency Bill necessary.'

'Mr Pitt is a politician. It is a politician's duty to conceive of such unpalatable things. I don't mind the Regency Bill, sir – I do mind your presumption in offering your unworthy self as Regent. Now pray do me the courtesy of departing.'

The King was himself again. Pitt rejoiced. London rejoiced. Frederick, Duke of York, rejoiced: for, as well as being genuinely fond of his father, he found himself more than ever in his father's good graces and, on promising to marry a German princess – any German princess would do – he had in return been promised a substantial addition to his income.

George, Prince of Wales, had only one cause for rejoicing: that his Maria had returned to him.

CHAPTER SEVEN

In the midst of all his turmoils the Prince had made time to resume his letter-writing. Once again he bombarded his love with appeals for mercy, poetic fantasies, protestations of undying devotion. The whole troublesome Fox misunderstanding was over and done with, people had other things to occupy their minds, she had discovered for herself that, so far from being ostracized by polite society, she was tacitly and sympathetically accepted as his wife. But how could she claim the acknowledgment of that if she were so obviously estranged from him? She must return and be in reality his own true wife.

No reply was received to any of his letters. But the indefatigable Colonel Lake, reporting as assiduously as any gossipy gazette on Mrs Fitzherbert's movements, hinted that a casual meeting might be contrived, so that face to face the two might settle their differences.

It came about on the terrace of the Duchess of Gordon's town house during a colourful, crowded soirée. He was alone with Maria, he touched her hand and kissed her averted cheek, talked, prevented her returning to the ballroom, went on his knees and went on pleading until she laughed in the way he loved best, and waved her fan protestingly; and then touched his lips with hers and surrendered.

'But,' she warned as they left in his coach, with his arm around her, impatient to have her back in his house and his bed, 'let us be clear on one thing, George. The rapture is gone.'

'No, no. Never. I love you so.'

'And I love you still. But I can never again trust you.'

Throughout the discussion of the possible Regency she

remained cool and aloof. He knew she suspected that he might now wish, after all, to abandon her: with such a prize dangling before him, to edge her discreetly into the background on the pretext that once he was so solidly in the public eye the old scandals might be raked up and she would suffer again.

'I appreciate your need for caution,' she said at one juncture. 'Only pray do not disguise it, George, as a sanctimonious concern for my well-being.'

But she was the first to weep when it was known that the King was fully restored and taking up the reins of administration again.

'You've been robbed, my sweet, of something you rightly deserved. The Regency would have been the making of you. But don't repine. You'll recover, you'll rise above this setback.' In her arms he was comfortable for hours, for a succession of healing, soothing nights. But then he felt the sting of injustice scorching him again. He needed to strike back at those who had wooed and then discarded him; needed to wrench free once and for all from his debts and troubles and frustrations. 'Come with me to Brighton,' Maria was urging gently. 'Let us see our friends once more, and become that happy couple we once were, comfortable and quiet . . .'

'No.' He broke the spell and stood back from her. 'I will not run away again. I will not live quietly.'

'You must. We must.'

'I am the Prince of Wales,' he thundered. 'I owe it to society, to the artists who need my patronage, to all that is beautiful and creative and noble, to *lead*, not to retreat. I will not stifle in Brighton. Or, if we do go there from time to time, then it will be to build on my little pavilion and transform it into a palace. Yes, that's what I want – to make a palace there, too.'

'Then you are doomed to a life of misery.'

'You don't love me.'

'You're maudlin drunk, or you wouldn't speak so. Love is allowed criticism.'

'I am the Prince of Wales, I'll not be spoken to — '

'You're also my drunken husband. And getting fat, with it. Fat and peevish. You want to poison your life and mine with it. Why did I come back to you, why did I sacrifice — '

'And what have I not sacrificed because of you?'

He was saying unpardonable things, and knew it, and was dizzy with an insane readiness to lash out as his insane father had done. No! He would not let himself. No . . .

'You must listen to me,' she implored.

'You are the cause of all my ills.' He could not believe it was his own voice he heard; and if it was not his own, how could he gag it? 'You've alienated me from my father, denied me the rights of my station . . .'

'You're talking about money again,' she said wearily.

'With money at least I could exercise the patronage this country needs. I could bring London up to the artistic level of Vienna, Paris – oh, far beyond.'

'We were happy' – she was looking into some far, lost distance – 'at Brighton.'

'Brighton is behind us. I must move on.'

Her attention came slowly, wistfully back to his face, reading in it things she already sensed. 'I know what's in your mind. You wish to follow in your brother's footsteps. A marriage – which would bring you money.'

'Oh, what nonsense, I — '

'George. Is it nonsense?'

'Well . . . oh, let's be sensible, would it be so bad? A marriage for money. And to please the people. You said yourself that I ought to be more popular with the people. So why not a marriage, a formality – a patriotic gesture? My heart would still be with you.'

He marvelled that she should still be studying him with such disdain. How could she not see the logic of it? An official residence and an official wife: and a cosy domestic hearth and loving wife elsewhere.

'You think I would connive at such a betrayal of my self and what I have been to you?'

'What would it signify?' he blustered. 'Some damned German frau or other – a marriage for the sake of my father, and Parliament, and the succession. Not a true marriage.'

She was too cruel, too unyielding. 'It's not good enough.'

'There has to be a compromise. In the nature of it there has to be. I accept that. Can't you do the same?'

'Never,' she said simply.

'Oh, damn it. And damn you, and damn love, and all your talk about love if you can call it love when you're so obdurate, so . . . so . . .'

'George, listen to me.' She was calm and implacable. 'I know you, my dear. I know well enough that you'll talk yourself into doing whatever it pleases you to do. But be assured that if you do *this* thing, I shall not this time return to you. Not this time, nor ever again.'

They were words, no more. She must know that it did not please him to do what he proposed. But marry he must, for reasons he had given and reasons he must know. And in the end she, too, would see reason.

'You'll marry?' said the King incredulously. 'Am I to understand that at last you're set on pleasing me?'

'To please your Majesty, I have now broken all connection with Mrs Fitzherbert. And I deem it incumbent on me to testify to the sincerity of my feelings by offering to sacrifice myself in any manner which your Majesty may think advisable.'

'Excellent,' marvelled his father. 'Excellent. So it remains only to choose who your wife shall be.'

'Since the future of England appears to depend on whether or not I settle accounts with my wine merchant and carpenters and plasterers, sir, then any damn German frau will do as well as another. As it did for Frederick.'

The King twitched, struck by a discordant note. But since his son had at last made such concessions, he would show regal generosity. 'Mm. Yes, what-what? There's my sister Augusta's girl. About the right age, and the Brunswick alliance . . . ah, yes. Mm.'

'I don't think Mama is too fond of the Brunswicks,' ventured the Prince.

'Your mother will know how to accept what's best for you, my boy. Yes,' said the King, enraptured, 'I will send Harris to Brunswick for the Princess Caroline. Harris will know exactly how to handle the matter.'

PART TWO

THE BRIDE FROM BRUNSWICK

CHAPTER ONE

James Harris, Earl of Malmesbury, had in his time been entrusted with many delicate assignments. He had been a shrewd ambassador to the court of St Petersburg, and then minister at the Hague. As the French Revolution sent ripples of fear through the vulnerable heads of kings and princelings throughout Europe, he moved from one country to another encouraging the formation of defensive alliances. When France, not content with a war against Austria and Prussia, arrogantly declared war on Britain and Holland also, Harris rushed to Berlin to link Prussian strategy with British. He kept a wary eye on the generalship of the Duke of York and on lukewarm allies. His skill in juggling a dozen diplomatic problems at once had been the reason for his elevation to the peerage. But few missions had taxed him so, or so dismayed him, as this one showed signs of doing.

He arrived in the duchy of Brunswick on a November afternoon in 1794. The weather had been cold and blustery during his journey, but the welcome at the ducal palace was warm enough. He was met by the chief of the Duke's cabinet and assured that an entire apartment had been put at his disposal, together with a valet, a concierge, three footmen, a carriage, and two sentries. Escorted up a splendid staircase and along a gallery hung with Brunswick family portraits, he savoured the ornate yet attractively small-scale dignity of the place.

The gravity was broken by a sudden screech and a tumult of giggling. Harris stopped, glancing through a half-open door to his left. Across the gap ran a young woman with tousled hair and flushed red face – reddened, perhaps, by her efforts to escape a young lieutenant who was driving her into a corner of the room. She hid behind a large armchair, then darted out again, steadied herself against a huge porcelain stove only to jerk away as the heat stung her palm, and fell into her pursuer's arms. Her squeal of protest was far from convincing. His hand tugged at the throat of her bodice, and from where Harris stood it looked as if she were dabbing greedily at the lieutenant's breeches.

Over his right epaulette the young woman's gaze suddenly met Harris's. She wrinkled her nose, but did not pull away from her captor. Embarrassed, Harris moved on. Decorum in the Brunswick palace apparently left much to be desired.

At table that evening he sat between the Duke and Duchess, each of whom wished to monopolize his attention. The Duke bumbled on in a stiff German accent about his plans for resisting the French, how he would have handled the defence of Holland if he had been in the King of Prussia's boots, how shamefully disorganized the Austrians were, and how simple the campaign could be made if only people would listen to him. The Duchess, delighted to have the chance of chattering away in English to a fellow countryman, gushed on deliriously about her daughter.

'You know of course, that all the young German princesses have been learning English in the hope of marrying the Prince of Wales. I never imagined it would be our Caroline who would be chosen. Never did I think — '

'It is my honour that is at stake, Excellency,' went on the Duke. 'Command a rabble of Austrians I will not. I — '

'Especially,' said the Duchess, 'as my brother the King so often expressed dislike of the idea of marriage with his German cousins.'

Harris ventured: 'The Princess will, I trust, be joining us this evening, Your Highness?'

'She's a little *en retard*. I'm sure she wishes to take particular pains with her toilette.'

'She is *late*,' said the Duke bluntly. 'Always we have

the trouble with her. So much trouble we take, and always she is headstrong, and again we must be strict and more strict. Believe me, Excellency, it has been necessary. Most necessary.'

Before Harris could summon up some platitude in reply, the doors were flung open and a young woman entered, followed by a flustered middle-aged lady who might have been a family retainer, nurse, or governess.

'There!' said the Duchess a shade too eagerly. 'Our daughter Caroline.'

Harris rose, touching his lips with his napkin. The young woman who swaggered across the room was not quite the poised princess he had been awaiting. She was the red-faced hoyden who had been fumbling with such appetite at the young lieutenant in that room near his suite. And she was still red in the face: not from the heat of the chase, nor from embarrassment, but simply from a natural high colouring and coarse skin.

'His Excellency, the Earl of Malmesbury,' his hostess was saying.

He swept a bow. '*Enchantée, Princesse.*'

In truth he was by no means enchanted. Nor, he feared, would the Prince of Wales be. This Princess Caroline was six years younger than her intended bridegroom, which made her twelve years younger than Mrs Fitzherbert. But her complexion was as rough as a fisher-girl's compared to that of the silky older woman. Harris's heart sank. He knew the Prince's tastes; and doubted that this gawky creature would arouse anything but distaste.

'How do you do.' Caroline's voice was as harsh as her skin. 'Lord Marmaladesbury? Ha, I can practise my English upon you.'

As he kissed her hand, Harris could hardly fail to notice something else which would enormously offend the fastidious Prince of Wales.

She stank.

When she was seated at table, the young woman leaned

roguishly forward to see what she could make of Harris, while the Duchess beamed both indulgently and apprehensively on behalf of this daughter whose marital hopes now surpassed all the family expectations.

The Duke said: 'Tomorrow, miss, the Milord will commence instruction on how one conducts oneself at Court in England.'

Caroline thrust out chapped red lips in an exaggerated pout. 'Then I must tell you, Milord, that I have not even made up my mind to take the Prince of Wales as husband. Already to the Prince of Orange I have said no.' She jabbed two fingers derisively in the air. 'Twice.'

'Enough!' growled her father.

'To the Prince of Prussia also. Once. And to the Prince of Darmstadt, who' – Caroline's tongue dabbed at her upper lip – 'was most pleasingly endowed.' She giggled: an echo of that giggle Harris had heard through a half-open door. 'Also,' said Caroline loudly, 'I have been told that the Prince only likes women when they are fair, fat and forty.'

'Will you stop this confounded chattering?' Her father thumped the table. 'Let us have the music. Oh, and also the dwarf – to entertain our most welcome visitor.'

Caroline reached across the table to a salad bowl, picked up a small onion with her fingers, and began to munch it loudly.

Harris was glad when it was time for bed; but it took him some time to go to sleep.

In the morning he wrote to the King and to the Prince of Wales. Tact was necessary. He thought of the lavishness of his welcome here, and wrote that as England's emissary he had been most courteously received. Without the Princess before his eyes, he tried to recall some of her more agreeable attributes: fair hair and light eyebrows, a good bust, all good nature and with what the French called *des épaules impertinentes*. It would be what the Prince wanted to hear.

His misgivings returned when Princess Caroline was

delivered into his charge so that he might devote the morning to instructing her in the graces her father enjoined.

She left him in no doubt about her own misgivings. 'Vastly happy about her future expectations,' he had written. But without preamble she said: 'I shall not be comfortable in England. No, not at all. There will be jealousy and suspicion all the time. And there is enough of that here.'

'Then may I suggest, Princess, that you spend some time with Her Majesty the Queen and allow her to be a model to you. In her dignity and affability — '

'Ah, I know all about the Queen. She does not like my mother, she does not wish me for her son.'

'You have been misinformed.'

'No, Lord Marmaladesbury. Oh, but I cannot call you that. I shall call you Harris.' Caroline jerked her head up at him as they strolled through the sunken garden. She tried a cheeky grin, to reveal teeth stained and uneven. 'And I tell you, Harris, that I know very well about my English relations. They are all terrible. My mother has told me so.'

'Her Highness has been away from England a long time. Probably she has forgotten a great deal.'

'But do not forget I have met the Prince's brother. The Duke of York was here. I was told once that he had perhaps thought of me for himself, but then he thought otherwise, and I suppose in England they all thought, "Ah, for the older brother this German will do".'

'I assure you,' said Harris, 'that such a thought could never for a moment enter anyone's mind.'

'Hah!'

She slapped him conspiratorially on the hip, and spun away from him. He winced, not at the blow but at the smell of her.

'Princess, it is my duty to commend to you . . .'

She turned to face him. 'Yes?'

'Discretion. No familiarity.'

'I am too familiar with you? You are not a true man, you do not like it?'

'Princess, you are to marry the heir to the English throne. You will need discretion . . . dignity. Perhaps just a little less talking, yes?'

'No talking? But in England I wish to be popular.'

'Quite. The love of a nation, however, can never be simply procured by mere pleasant openess.'

'I am "open"?' Caroline sniggered lewdly.

Harris tried to keep step with her – to establish a grave, graceful pace while they talked – but she lunged this way and that, grimaced over each phrase, and every now and then ran grubby fingers through her tangled hair.

'A lady's affability,' he tried again, 'should never deteriorate to a level of over-familiarity.'

'I am also "familiar"?' Flouncing ahead of him, she spoke quietly into nowhere; then swung back and shouted at the top of her voice: 'It is the trouble with we Brunswickers, yes? Admit it – you do not think we are proper. Not proper. Not fit for your Windsor, your London.'

'Princess, I was merely endeavouring — '

'Try some other German courts, then! The Margrave of Baden he keep a harem of actresses. My cousin Augustus of Saxony, often he makes the orgies. The Margravine of Bayreuth-Kumbach introduces her lovers into her daughter's bed. *I* have been brought up as strictly as a nun. But I am not proper, not respectable enough for your so-proper Prince of Wales?'

She veered away. Harris chased after her at an undignified trot.

As if to appease her, or somehow to appease fate without her direct knowledge, he wrote again to London to say how the Princess Caroline improved on acquaintance: so gay and cheerful and eager to please. The King had at no time asked that even in the most confidential, diplomatic way Harris should hint whether or not Caroline was truly fit to be Princess of Wales. His commission had not included the task of expressing criticisms or forebodings. He was charged only with settling the marriage contract and escorting the bride-to-be back to England.

The Prince of Wales was now issuing urgent demands. He was impatient to meet his Princess. Reading between the lines, Harris suspected that this was not so much a lover's impatience as a wish to get the whole thing over and done with, and collect the money.

Prompt departure in answer to this royal summons was no easy matter. With war rolling to and fro across Europe, it was necessary to wait for a lull. And even then they would have to choose an indirect route to avoid the inspired sorties of French detachments.

In the meantime he occupied himself and his charge with further discussions on her future conduct and what she might expect in her new homeland.

Still the young woman remained perkily argumentative, all too often taking the initiative and hectoring him rather than consulting him.

'Your Prince of Wales, is he not *un peu léger*? He is fickle, no?'

'It is with her own duties and steadfast attitude that a Princess of Wales should concern herself.'

'He keeps the mistresses. Yes or no?'

'It would be wise not to listen to the tittle-tattle of ladies of the Court.'

'Ah, yes, I hear of the ladies of the Court. I hear many of them go into the Prince's bed. And a certain Mrs Fitzherbert — '

'My dear Princess, reproaches will never claim or reclaim a husband's affections. The surest way of retaining them is by softness, by sympathy and by caresses. Jealousy, on the other hand — '

'Oh, do not be anxious on that account, Harris. It is not my intention to be jealous. Already I know of love and its — '

'Please!' Harris did not want to be in receipt of any scandalous confidences.

'I speak of my father,' she said, more gently than usual. 'It has been difficult for me at *this* Court. I love my father, but he has three ladies to love. Most of all he is attached to a Madame de Hertzfeldt – you know?'

'I met the lady, many years ago. Before she . . . um . . .'

'My mother is not angry, because my father also pays all possible respect to her. But between my mother and Madame de Hertzfeldt I never know what to do. When I am civil to one, I am scolded by the other. So I am tired of both of them. But, Harris, I have learned that jealousy is of little use.'

They were standing close together, in that very room where he had once glimpsed her disporting herself with the young lieutenant. Harris felt moved by her naïve confidences. Then he saw a tempting, speculative gleam in her eye; and backed away in alarm. Surely she could not be contemplating . . . not, surely, with him . . .?

That proximity reminded him of another distasteful matter. Her coarse shift, her thread stockings, the unfashionable and unwashed gowns, the unwashed skin . . .

He hesitated between the Duchess and Madame de Hertzfeldt; and chose Madame de Hertzfeldt.

'Madame, your tact could be of the greatest value in putting one point to the Princess. The Prince of Wales is very delicate in his perceptions. If you really mean well by Her Highness, you might find some way of suggesting to her that the Prince always expects the most careful *toilette de propreté* from a lady.'

He hoped he was not too obviously ill at ease.

Madame de Hertzfeldt, herself ageing but with that well-groomed appearance and perennially youthful complexion which could not but remind one of Mrs Fitzherbert, feigned astonishment.

'Are you saying that the Princess does not wash with sufficient care?'

'It's remarkable how this aspect of her education has been neglected, and how inattentive her mother, though an Englishwoman, is to it.'

Madame de Hertzfeldt mused for a moment. Then she wagged her head. 'Let us be frank, my friend. Caroline is not only destitute of all female delicacy, she is an extremely loose little baggage who will dally with the first little courtier who comes to hand.'

'I agree that Her Highness's education is by no means finished, but — '

'If she is allowed to marry the Prince of Wales,' said Madame de Hertzfeldt with sudden, frightening fervour, 'it will be a disaster. Can you not see it? A disaster!'

CHAPTER TWO

Messages from England grew peremptory. At the end of December came an explicit order from the King that Harris should accompany the Princess without more ado to the island of Texel, off the Dutch coast, where a British naval escort would be awaiting them. There was a great to-do, a flurry of preparation, a frenzy of packing and planning during the day followed by toasts and congratulations each evening. As a token of his esteem the Duke of Brunswick gave Harris a beautifully enamelled snuff-box. The Princess Caroline herself surprised and touched him by summoning a lackey with a prettily wrapped package which she insisted he open in her presence.

'For me?' Harris felt a glow of affection for this absurd, impulsive, but so unquenchably generous girl. 'I am most touched. Most grateful.' He began to open the wrappings.

'Wear it around your neck when we depart for England,' said Caroline.

How sentimental the funny little creature was!

Harris opened the tiny box within, and stared at its contents – a small, uneven, slightly yellowing object with a dark chip across one end. 'Most grateful,' he repeated uncertainly. 'That is . . . er, what exactly is it?'

The shriek of laughter which he had vainly hoped to subdue came screeching out again. 'A tooth, my dear Harris! One of mine! I had it drawn from my mouth before breakfast. Keep it as a token of my profound thanks for all your patience and commendations.'

She was, he feared, incurable.

Three days later their carriage set off. It bore not only the Princess and her escort but the Princess's mother, determined to go as far as the coast from which her sweet, soaring, successful girl would embark. Harris could well have done without the Duchess Augusta's chatter; but was offered no choice.

His pessimism about the journey was justified. Through searing cold they managed during several days to weave a way round battle salients and rumours of battle, until they reached Osnabruck. Here the tides of conflict threatened to cut them off; and there was no confirmation that the promised British ships were where they ought to have been. After four days of marking time, despatches recommended continuing the journey. But almost as soon as it had been resumed, conflicting despatches followed to suggest they should turn back before being encircled by the French. They lived through more days of biting frost at Osnabruck; Harris continued to instruct Princess Caroline in the niceties of deportment at the English Court, wondering if they would ever reach it; and then they were forced to take shelter in Hanover, where the Duchess was in her element among old friends and relatives.

Not until March did Harris thankfully shed the maudlin, gossipy mother and set off yet again with his charge. His hopes of having by now achieved some stabilization of the Princess's erratic moods and foibles received a setback when, after jolting interminable miles along the bumpy, unpredictable roads, she thrust before him a letter addressed to the Duchess.

'Mama gave me this before we left.'

Harris skimmed down it and felt a prickle of cold horror across the back of his neck. The anonymous scrawl warned the Duchess that her daughter would be marrying a man already in the toils of a liaison with 'the most profligate and dangerous of women' in England.

'Exceedingly indiscreet of your mother,' Harris temporized.

'But it is all true, no?'

'I do not for one moment suppose — '

'Is she the Prince's mistress, this' – Caroline snatched the letter back – 'this Lady Jersey? Yes or no?'

If Frances, Countess of Jersey, was indeed now the Prince's favourite, it was news to Harris. The relationship must have blossomed during his protracted absence. Presumably, having discarded Mrs Fitzherbert, the Prince of Wales had sought temporary distraction elsewhere until his bride should arrive from Brunswick.

Harris said: 'One does not, your Highness, pay attention to this sort of letter. Clearly it is the work of some disappointed maidservant.'

'If it is true, though, what kind of life may *I* expect? How am *I* to be entertained? If he is so busy with his other woman, then where may *I* busy myself?'

'The suggestion that Lady Jersey's conduct – if there be such conduct – would ever enable your Highness to embark upon a . . . an . . .'

'An affair of gallantry? Why not? The Prince he has them, so they must be proper, and you are so anxious I should be proper.'

'It is death,' insisted Harris, 'even to presume to approach a Princess of Wales.'

'You mean no man would ever dare to make love with me?'

'He would be found guilty of high treason and sent to the gallows.'

'And she? I mean, me?' When he made no answer, she stared in mounting disbelief, and whispered: 'Death?'

'Certainly.' He made it as emphatic and final as he could. 'If she were ever weak enough to succumb to such deplorable temptation.'

'Oh, what a pity.'

The coach lurched and Caroline was thrown against him. She made no move to right herself, but looked up at him with widening, mocking eyes.

'Washed all over!' she taunted him. 'You see, I do care for what you say.'

Stricken, he disentangled himself and edged back into the corner of his seat, away from her touch but not from that triumphant little belch of laughter.

He was infinitely relieved when this time, at last, they were met and carried safely by Hanoverian ship to a rendezvous with the waiting British squadron.

Aboard the *Jupiter*, surrounded by deferential British officers and the panoply of state which was now her due, Caroline wallowed – rather too exuberantly for Harris's taste – in conversation and the men's admiration. Her high spirits endeared her to the crew. So, also, they did to Harris, however much he might fight against it. For all her gaucheness and brashness he had come to like her openness of heart, the lack of any shadow of pride or self-consciousness. She was so good-humoured and devoid of art. But those were gifts little likely, he thought glumly, to commend her to the Prince. As they drew closer to the mouth of the Thames he grew hourly more apprehensive.

The last stage of the voyage seemed to take an eternity. Thick fog had settled over the coast and the estuary, and they were many hours late in finding the royal yacht which was to carry the Princess along the last stretch to Greenwich.

By the time they moored before the creamy splendour of the Royal Hospital, the sun was out. This ought to have been a good omen; but there was an omen of a different kind in the absence of the avowedly impatient Prince. Guns thundered a salute. A troop of dragoons made a fine splash of colour along the waterfront. But there was no royal reception party.

'Well, Harris? Where are they – the King, the so handsome Prince of Wales, the royal carriages?'

Caroline had, he noted with approval, done her best to provide a fetching first impression. She wore a muslin dress over a blue satin petticoat, and a tasselled gold-trimmed satin mantle lay easily about her shoulders. Her black beaver hat, sprouting blue and black feathers, was perhaps a trifle too jaunty; but it was so much a part of her, so much in keeping, that he had not the heart to make even the most tentative criticism.

'The fog has probably caused confusion elsewhere. If Her Highness will exercise a little patience — '

'Patience? When the Prince sees fit to send not so much as a . . .' Her voice trailed away as a carriage came at a spanking pace on to the quay by the end of the gangplank. 'Who is this?'

A small woman with a complexion like the smoothest, most delicate veneer came aboard, flanked by two ladies-in-waiting. She bowed deeply, then smiled up into the Princess's face. It was a feline, sardonic little smile: she had all the grace and inner complacency of a pampered cat, and her deep eyes had a golden cat-like glow.

'Lady Jersey,' said Harris. 'We were not expecting you.'

'Your Royal Highness,' purred Lady Jersey, 'welcome to England. I have had the honour to be appointed Lady of the Bedchamber to your Royal Highness.'

'Appointed? By — '

'By Her Majesty the Queen.'

How could the man have let it happen? How could he have permitted such an insult to be offered just as Princess Caroline was about to set foot on English soil for the first time? Harris despaired. He was also somewhat taken aback by this latest choice of royal mistress. The Prince had never before shown any predilection for women so petite. But still, the fact that she was a grandmother accorded with what all the malicious tongues forever said of him.

Harris stepped aside so that the Princess might precede them ashore. There was another crashing salute of guns, and somewhere a band began to play.

As they reached the waiting carriage, Lady Jersey turned to Harris and said brightly: 'Oh, your Grace. Before we set off for London I must tell you, I cannot bear to sit with my back to the horses. It makes me ill.'

'I grieve to hear it.'

'I would therefore deem it a favour if I could sit beside the Princess.'

This was the ultimate outrage. Harris barked out: 'That, I regret to tell her Ladyship, would constitute a most serious breach of etiquette.'

'Oh, come now . . .'

'Yes.' It was an abrupt, harsh cry from Caroline. Hands on hips, she looked like a flushed washerwoman about to start a heated argument. 'You tell her, Harris!'

The harness of the dragoons jingled and then was silent, as if the whole troop wanted to hear what was going on.

Harris kept his voice down. 'If riding backwards in a carriage is so disagreeable to her Ladyship, she would have been well advised not to accept the position of Lady of the Bedchamber.'

'I solicit advice,' said Lady Jersey, with a hint of claws coming out, 'only from the Prince of Wales himself.'

'So I gather, ma'am, so I gather.' Harris turned and bowed the Princess towards the carriage step. 'Your Royal Highness, if you please.'

The journey into the capital was far from comfortable, but fortunately as news of the Princess's approach ran ahead, people came flocking out of houses and side streets, and welcoming cheers and shouts washed over the awkward silence within the coach.

They were driven to the palace of St James's on which crowds were already converging. A window was thrown up so that Caroline might show herself to the populace, and the spontaneous roars of welcome brought even higher colour to her cheeks. When she backed away into the room again, she ventured a smile at Harris. He smiled reassuringly back.

Lady Jersey said: 'And now, before it pleases Her Royal Highness to appear before the Prince of Wales, we shall do well to make certain adjustments. For a beginning, Her Royal Highness will wish to edify her face after what appears to have been an excessively rough crossing. Come, ladies – powder and rouge.'

Before the Princess could protest, two other women had pressed her back into a chair and were dabbing at her face. At the same time Lady Jersey, walking round her with pursed lips, was observing:

'As for that . . . garment . . . it would appear more suited to a country frolic than a royal reception. No, we must change into a dress more appropriate to the occasion. Ladies!'

Another cohort of ladies-in-waiting advanced on Caroline with a white satin dress and a feathered turban.

'No!' she burst out. 'I will not have such a hat. My hat was made for me by the best milliner in Brunswick. Do what else you like, but my hat I shall keep.'

Lady Jersey contrived a delicate little shrug. Harris would willingly have struck her. But there had been enough trouble already; and he feared more for this poor, silly, doomed young woman.

Outside there was a swell of cheering, mixed with a few catcalls, and then a clatter of hoofs and carriage wheels.

The Prince of Wales had arrived to greet his intended bride.

Princess Caroline looked imploringly at Harris for succour. He smiled again, with more confidence than he actually felt, and went to the reception room where the Prince waited.

'Well, Harris. Mission almost completed, ha? I must congratulate you. Most obliged to you.'

The apprehension Harris had suffered on the Princess's behalf was redoubled. In all these last difficult months he had been single-mindedly concerned about the young woman's appearance, her speech, her deportment, her effect on the Prince of Wales. It had somehow been relegated to the back of his mind that the Prince was quite what he was. Now, for the first time, he wondered what impression George would make on *her*.

The Prince of Wales was resplendent in hussar uniform. It was something he could once have carried well. Now he carried too much else besides. He was over seventeen stone; and he bulged. His cheeks and jowls sagged, his belly sagged; and his calves swelled over the tops of his short Hessian boots.

Florizel had, over the years, become Falstaff.

'Well then, Harris, enough of the diplomacy. Where *is* the woman?'

Harris backed away and indicated to the flunkeys that the doors should be thrown open wide.

'If His Royal Highness will permit – Her Highness the Princess Caroline of Brunswick.'

In her white satin and incongruous hat, Caroline entered at a demure tread which Harris could not have faulted. He held is breath. She advanced upon the Prince, keeping her eyes respectfully down, and knelt before him.

'Your Royal Highness.'

The Prince took a step forward and raised her to him. He looked into her clownishly made-up face; and she into his.

Harris could see and almost feel her instinctive, incredulous shudder.

The Prince released her. Then, as if he had lost all sense of direction, he went blundering helplessly off into the farthest corner of the room.

Caroline, frozen where she stood, watched him go.

'Harris!'

'Your Royal Highness.' Harris followed across the room. 'Is there something amiss?'

There was a catch of breath in the Prince of Wales's throat. Words retched out of him:

'I am not at all well, Harris. Pray get me a glass of brandy.'

CHAPTER THREE

George, Prince of Wales, was riding with his brother William – riding out from London, out to Richmond, riding fiercely as if to flee the doom he had brought on himself. He sobbed as he went.

'William, what have I done?'

The Duke of Clarence shook his head in commiseration, but was in reality too much the bluff sailor to exude the right air of melancholy required by his brother. His own life so far had been direct, boisterous, and happy: he had ridden over or through troubles as if fearlessly steering a man-o'-war into whatever wave or gale might threaten. Having recently settled into cheerful if unsanctified domesticity with his hard-working actress, Mrs Jordan, he was content that the miseries and formal responsibilities of the realm should be shouldered by the Prince of Wales.

'My Maria,' cried George to the unresponsive air. 'My ever-beloved Maria!'

They reined in before Mrs Fitzherbert's gracious compact little Richmond house. The shutters were drawn, though the Prince had every reason to believe that his morganatic wife was at home.

He gazed up at that unyielding façade. 'William, will she ever forgive me?'

The Duke of Clarence fidgeted in his saddle. He had always been straightforward, always hateful of complexity. 'It grows chilly,' was the best he could offer. 'We must return.'

George could not force his attention away from those hooded, blank windows, so incongruous a barrier between him and the hooded but always languorously responsive eyes of his Maria. He remembered Park Street; remembered the little annexe at Brighton; remembered too much; and, to his terror, knew there was no way of ever forgetting.

'I must speak to her. I must.'

'No.' This at least had the power to wake William up. 'Exceeding ill-advised.'

'I must tell Maria everything.'

'You've told her already, old fellow. Told her it's over, and you're marrying because it's your duty and because you were born to that sort of thing, and there we are, eh?'

George was trying to force himself to turn his mount's head back towards London, towards the Mall and Carlton House and the preparations for tomorrow's ceremony. He must steel himself to go through with it all. No retraction was possible now.

He knew it; and thought of his cruelly dismissed Maria.

Why should the most gifted, most lovable, most loving and most eligible Christian Prince in all Europe be so ill used? There had been a hideous mistake, but not of his making. Not mine, he cried inwardly. If the wife of his heart were to send one soothing word, he would not be within miles of loathsome St James's tomorrow.

'George.' It was his brother, attempting in his clumsy way a soothing gesture. 'Let me see her for you. Some courtesy . . . something, hmp?'

'Will you? Yes, very well. Tell her . . .' It had been told before, it was ridiculous that someone else should have to convey the selfsame message now. He would storm the house, tear down the shutters, bring down the throne, let the temple fall about his ears. No one and no desperate need should persuade him to give up his Maria. He thought of what was waiting for him in London, tomorrow and all the thousands of tomorrows and tomorrows. 'Tell her,' he choked, 'that she's the only woman I shall ever love.'

As the Duke of Clarence rode with some trepidation towards the house, the Prince of Wales wheeled his horse around and trotted disconsolately off in the direction of his frightful destiny.

He would never forgive the Earl of Malmesbury. Never. Such a sly, suave diplomat: knowing whence came his honours, and careful never to tell an uncomfortable truth. Harris, the hypocrite: Harris, who had not once had the courage or compassion to tell either the King or the King's son that the proposed Princess of Wales was a stinking sloven with breath like that of a sewer and skin like a rotting medlar.

The wedding took place on the evening of 8th April 1795 in the Chapel Royal of St James's Palace. The altar was radiant with candles, the air was clamorous with the fanfare of trumpets, and a celebratory anthem had been composed for the occasion. Church bells pealed throughout the land. Hideous discords resounded through the head of the Prince of Wales.

'Dearly beloved, we are gathered here in the sight of God to join together this man and this woman . . .'

George felt his flabby knees beginning to give way. On either side, the Dukes of Bedford and of Roxburgh braced their feet and continued to support him. He had not had enough to drink: there ought surely to have been another bottle before he plodded in to face this ordeal.

Behind him he heard a shuffling, a whispering, a mockery of voices from those who eternally wished him ill and now had come to gloat over their reward.

Beside him was Princess Caroline of Brunswick.

Had she been compulsively nibbling onions again, just before the ceremony?

Brandy might smell; but it smelt better than onions.

The Archbishop of Canterbury was staring full at him. And was not merely intoning, but thrusting straight at the Prince: 'If any man can show any just cause why they may not be lawfully joined together, let him now speak, or else hereafter for ever hold his peace.'

I have only to speak, thought George. There is only

Maria, there can never be another wife but Maria, I have only to say it and be done with it, and drive this foul creature from my side, and devil take them all . . .

The yoke of more than six hundred thousand pounds lay about his neck. Could this new yoke possibly be heavier? It had already been agreed that the weight could be mollified.

'George Augustus, Prince of Wales, will thou have this woman to thy wedded wife . . .'

Maria – oh, Maria!

'Wilt thou love her, comfort her . . .'

I will, he wept in silence: God help me, I will try.

Choir and trumpets and peals of bells; fanfares, feasting and wild dancing in the streets; and insinuating romantic serenades at table, until the musicians and guests began to yawn and wonder when the Prince would ever take his bride to bed.

Tonight there was no drive towards a little retreat in Surrey. No frivolous escapade, no laughs in the Hammersmith tavern while the wheel of the coach was repaired. Nothing but the tactful, withdrawn silence of Carlton House: deserted corridors, servants invisible, amorous thoughts kindling in the pregnant air.

George sat alone and emptied a bottle of claret. Then reached for another.

Fox ought to be here, Sherry ought to be here. They ought to be laughing, encouraging him, lovingly persuading him that everything might still, by some miracle, be magnificent.

He must get up. Must force himself to go to his bride.

George went out, vomited, and came back for another bottle.

It was long, long past midnight when at last he summoned up the courage to go to his wife's bedroom. It took him a few seconds to get a good grip on the knob of the door. When he twisted it open, and looked at the bed and the contents of the bed, he thought that there must be another bottle, somewhere, which might just conceivably make the picture more palatable.

'Good evening, sir,' said that appalling voice.

It took him a long, vertiginous minute to reply. 'Goo'-night, ma'am.' He managed to close the door and walk towards the fireplace; and then found that he was swaying towards the bed.

'Is it not the custom in England, sir, to undress before one retires to bed?'

'It is, ma'am, it is. Frequently. Er . . . when one chooses to do so.'

'And pray' – oh, how that grating sound gouged through his head and bowels! – 'in England one shares one's bed with one's bride on one's wedding night, yes?'

'One does, madam, one does.'

He forced himself to contemplate that deplorable head and the shoulders which had been described to him as saucy but which he found coarse and unappetizing. But this marriage had to be consummated. He would have to close his eyes and pretend. On whom should he fix his imagination: Lady Jersey, curled up like a sportive kitten, or the plump little country wench he had fondled last week in the Windsor castle laundry . . . or Maria Fitzherbert?

He groaned, seized a poker, and began aimlessly stirring the lukewarm ashes in the grate.

'Kindly get undressed and come to bed,' she was rasping. 'You are not likely to produce an heir, sir, by watching the fire.'

Despite the throbbing in his head, the Prince straightened up manfully. From here his wife was no more than a blur in the bedclothes.

'Rest assured, madam. The Prince of Wales never shirks his duties, however onerous they may be. I will most certainly attend to you . . . in the morning.'

'In the morning, sir, *I* shall be asleep.'

He stooped to replace the poker, swaying over the grate. Suddenly she snatched her prayer-book from the bedside table and threw it so that, pages fluttering, it caught him behind the left ear and tipped him off balance. He went down in a clatter of fire-irons and a cloud of grey dust, sprawling across the fireplace and lying there unable to summon up the will to rise from the ashes.

CHAPTER FOUR

In Windsor Great Park the night air was bright with fireworks, crackling with the hiss and bang of rockets and set pieces and with the chatter of the onlookers. It was the Queen's birthday. As many of her family as could be assembled were here to share the evening; and a number of Privy Councillors, Guards officers, and favoured Members of Parliament had called at intervals to pay their respects. William Pitt was with her and the King. Charles Fox, favoured by neither, was closeted indoors with the Prince of Wales.

On the terrace, the Princess, helping herself from a tray of beer and pickled onions, grinned wickedly past the affronted Lady Jersey at the Duke of Clarence.

'The English,' she announced proudly, 'have not paid me a visit this month.'

Her attention was distracted for a moment by a flunkey passing with a bowl of nuts. She grabbed a handful and began to crunch them.

'The English?' said Lady Jersey, uncomprehending.

'In Europe this thing what we women have . . .' Caroline spluttered on a mouthful, tried to chisel an awkward fragment from between her teeth, and dropped one nut down the wide neck of her dress. Chuckling gleefully, she fished it out with her forefinger and offered it to her Lady of the Bedchamber, who flinched away. 'This thing we have every month,' she resumed, 'we call it the English. And that will tell you in all truth what we think of you and your country!'

'Are you trying to tell me, your Royal Highness — '

'That I am pregnant. Yes, that is what I tell you.'

While indoors, the Prince of Wales strode up and down

the small drawing-room clutching his paunch and crying: 'Never again! Never! Now that I have put my wife in a condition, I will never befoul myself again by so much as touching her with tongs, let alone by lying in her bed.'

'News of an heir could do much to make the people more friendly towards you,' observed Fox.

'Friendly? By God, Charles I can do with some friends.' George stared accusingly at his old companion. 'This news from the House – Charles, what do you think you're doing to me?'

'Working in your best interests, sir.'

'Deucedly strange way to go about it. The worst enemy a man ever had, Billy Pitt, puts a motion to the House raising my income to one hundred and twenty-five thousand, and you – *you*, who call yourself my friend – you have to propose an amendment whereby the government takes sixty-five thousand of it back again.'

'For the more rapid repayment of your debts.'

'To hell with my debts.'

'Half a million pounds cannot so lightly be consigned to hell.'

'I am abused. Betrayed.' The Prince turned to a side-board on which a dozen bottles of brandy and a dozen of claret had been laid out. He poured a brandy but did not offer one to Fox. 'How could you attempt to reduce my allowance? I have the right to more money, not less.'

Fox rubbed his eyes wearily. It was useless explaining to the Prince that this was the worst possible time to ask for an increase in his personal allowances, when the British people were so heavily taxed and being asked for so many other sacrifices. The war was not going well. Saxony, Hanover and the Palatinate were making terms with France, and Pichegru's troops were being daringly and skilfully deployed throughout Europe. British forces had landed in Quiberon to assist a Royalist revolt against the Republic; but it was a desperate throw unlikely to succeed, and else-where naval forces were perilously stretched from the

Indian Ocean to the Caribbean, at the same time having to keep watch along the Channel coast. At home there were bad harvests and high prices, men were being taken from their homes to strengthen the militia, harsh new laws against sedition and public meetings had been introduced, and the provisions of the Habeas Corpus act suspended, which led to further unrest. In this climate, what would the public make of a Prince who was over six hundred thousand pounds in debt and who now clamoured for more money with which to indulge his passions?

True, he had incurred new obligations – his wife, and now the promise of a child. And true, he would genuinely have been glad to lead an army into battle against the enemy and if necessary die for his country. He did buy expensive colourful silk waistcoats a dozen at a time; and he did gamble the night and his money away at White's all too often. But he had also amassed, as much for the nation as for himself, a great collection of fine works of art, and could plead that the expenditure on Carlton House was a non-recurring sum, since work was now virtually completed. All that, thought Fox ruefully, was plausible enough provided one did not know – as he knew – of the treasures stuffed away in attics because the impulsive purchases had failed to please the Prince by the time they were delivered.

No, this was no time for the Prince of Wales to plead poverty before his countrymen.

Fox said: 'Don't you see, if Pitt's proposals go through, he and your father will have you in debt for the rest of your life. It's a plot between them, to keep you entirely dependent on them.'

'I don't understand.'

'Pitt has ruled, with your father's connivance, that only twenty-five thousand pounds should be deducted annually from your allowance to pay off your debts. If we add to this a compound interest of four per cent, you won't be able to discharge those debts for another twenty-seven years.'

'Twenty-seven years?' groaned the Prince.

'The whole nation can now read the Parliamentary report. Every tradesman in the land knows that your credit is, to say the least, not good. Should you now try to purchase so much as a snuff-box or handkerchief, they'll know they're going to have to wait a very long time for repayment.'

'Twenty-seven years,' repeated the Prince, awe-struck.

'At least that. And I'm afraid it's likely to be worse.'

'How could it be worse?'

'That malicious abomination, Mr Pitt, glossed over his "four per cent" as though it were of no great consequence. But where on the market can you borrow at four per cent today? Or even five per cent? With this French war, rates will soon be eight, nine, or ten per cent. So, giving my most optimistic estimate' – Fox fished from his pocket the paper on which he had been jotting figures during the drive to Windsor – 'I can't see you being free of debt for another hundred and fifty-eight years.'

'Charles, this is madness. What am I to do?'

'It's rather a matter of what we can persuade your father to do. Knowing the people's adversity and their probable antagonism to any Parliamentary concession on your behalf, I did suggest that His Majesty should help clear your liabilities out of his own purse.'

It was not, Fox admitted to himself, the likeliest way to win royal approval. Nor would the King have looked too kindly on his reminder to the House of the execution of King Louis XVI. 'Is it wise,' he had insinuated, 'in these troubled times to suffer kings and princes to be known only to their people by expenses and taxes?' Let the matter be settled honourably and swiftly. He had put it to the House, and through the House to the nation, that the Prince of Wales had never been fairly dealt with and was not to be condemned for his difficulties. By Act of Parliament he should have received from birth, instead of only after his majority, all the revenues of the Duchy of Cornwall – which had instead been appropriated by his father, supposedly for the Prince's education.

'My speech has been reported in The Times,' said Fox now. 'You will have every sympathy.'

'Who cares about sympathy? Where's my money?'

'Apparently some two million pounds of it,' said Fox, 'was spent on your education, as I said in my speech.'

'Two million? On my education?' The Prince groped for another bottle from the sideboard, brushing aside Fox's attempt to coax him away. 'Education? Nothing but religion and the whip. All my childhood he had me dressed in girls' frocks, with tucks and hems and bodices – and my tutors were encouraged five or six times a day to lift up my skirts and flog me like a dog.'

'I know, I know.'

'Lud, Charlie, the wonder is not that I've slept with so many women but that I've gone to bed with any at all.' The Prince took down half the contents of a glass at one gulp. 'And now where am I? The way you're behaving, I'll finish up as a married man with less than was my due when I became twenty-one.'

Fox nodded. He had already worked out this depressing calculation, too.

'What am I to do?' wept the Prince. 'Have I no one to turn to?'

CHAPTER FIVE

The Prince of Wales sat at his writing desk in Carlton House penning a letter to his father. His eyes were red with tiredness and his hand was unsteady, as it had been for some hours now; but the dutiful missive would be expected of him, and he was too exhausted to contemplate facing any further antagonism from the King.

> The Princess, after a terrible hard labour for about twelve hours is this day brought to bed of an immense girl, and I assure you, notwithstanding we might have wished for a boy, I received her with all the affection possible, and bow with due deference and resignation to the decrees of Providence.

There was a tap at the door, which opened to admit a deferential Lord Jersey.

'My most joyous felicitations, your Royal Highness.'

The Prince heaved his aching bulk out of the chair and laid a heavy hand on his visitor's shoulder. 'Ah, it has been a most fearful trial and strain. Twelve long hours of labour pains! I do not think I could face such an ordeal again. Altogether too gruelling.'

Along the Mall there was a sudden crash of cannon fire. As if his sufferings were not enough, the Royal Artillery had to join in! Was there no mercy?

He was holding his head wretchedly between his hands as another salute was fired, as if to announce Lady Jersey, entering the room behind her husband.

'My poor dear.' She came to slide the Prince's hands gently away from his ears and guide them to her waist. 'How are you, my dear Prince?'

Her light blue chemise robe, with its low décolletage, was filmy and almost transparent; and there were not too many buttons to impede thick, impatient fingers.

'Lord Jersey,' said the Prince, 'I do find your wife's presence most comforting.'

Lord Jersey bobbed an obsequious bow. 'I have great joy in the knowledge that both my wife and I can be of personal service to you.'

'You're most affable, my dear man, most affable. And now might I ask you to deliver these letters I have just written? One to His Majesty . . . here, I must sign it.' He scrawled across the bottom of the paper, sanded it, and folded it. 'And pray leave me to your dear lady a while.'

'Our obedience in all things, your Royal Highness.'

When Lord Jersey had gone, the Prince allowed his hand to rove more freely. 'Most understanding person, your husband.'

'We are your servants, my dearest.' Her head drooped against his chest.

'Then serve me by getting me to bed. And put me to sleep, as you alone know how.'

'Such is my abundant privilege,' she said tenderly.

So musical a voice, so softly cooing a voice: so different from that abominable squawk, that affront to the human hearing. George nearly put his hands over his ears again. But once in his bedroom, with the door firmly closed, he heard nothing but what the delicious, devoted Frances was murmuring to him.

They lay there for a good two hours, in daylight dimmed by the long curtains. Once, far away along the Mall, there was an outburst of cheering. Peals of bells sang faintly, spasmodically in from different parts of the city. But he was relaxed now: soothed, saved, finding reasons for being pleased with what he had achieved.

'All is resolved.' He swung his legs out of bed and reached for his gold-frogged brocade dressing-gown. 'I have produced an heir to the British throne.'

'Yes, my dear Georgie. But it's a girl, remember.'

'What of it? Have we not had a Queen Anne and a Queen Elizabeth? Oh, I fancy I've done my duty by the British nation. Let them be grateful.' He slapped his thigh. 'Lud be praised! I've just remembered: I've won a wager with Sherry. I've gotten me a child before him. I must send a messenger round to Brooks's to collect the loot.'

'Do you think he'll pay up?'

'He'd better, or I'll have the Lord Chamberlain ban all his plays.'

Yes, this was a good day, a most auspicious day.

Lady Jersey turned drowsily over in bed. 'You'll have to make a public appearance soon. The people will want to see you as a father, holding the child.'

This had not so far occurred to him. But of course the dear woman was right. Their future King must be seen presenting their future Queen to the nation. Yes, he must plan it: a colourful ceremony, perhaps a special uniform designed by himself so that the populace could see how seriously he took his country's military standing; and perhaps an entire new balcony or garden terrace for Carlton House so that on future occasions they might have a better view of himself and his growing daughter.

'I think I'll go along the corridor and have a look at the infant,' he said.

'What will you say to your wife? You haven't spoken to her since the birth.'

'I shall say, "Thank you kindly, madam, you've done your task." After all, I can afford to be kind to her now. As soon as she's recovered I'll be putting her out to grass. Somewhere in the country. The further the better.'

'Taking the baby with her?'

The Prince turned in the doorway. 'Frances, do you suppose for one moment that I'd leave my child in the care of that bitch?'

'Don't affront her. She could be dangerous.'

'I shall be even-tempered, I promise you, in the hope of her early departure.'

'She'll do well in the privacy of the country. There she might satisfy her cravings.'

Her cravings! The Prince went out, not trusting himself to speak. That slobbering fiend – let her have men, let her take her smell to a farmyard and entice any ignorant yokel she could find, so long as he never had to clap eyes on her again. Until then, though, he must be as sweet as sugar.

All the way along the corridors he rehearsed the pleasant things he would say to her, the courteous nothingnesses which would not be too hard to utter, the compromises he proposed to suggest when the moment was right.

It was only when he saw her again that he realized how difficult it would be to act convincingly. As he entered the bedroom, where a wet nurse was feeding the baby, Caroline was propped up in bed chewing a long German sausage and letting odd globules of grease fall on a letter open on the quilt before her.

'My dear Caroline.' He tried resolutely to play his part. 'How are you feeling?'

'*Gut. Zeh gut.*' She held out the sausage. 'You want a bite?'

'Thank you, no. And how is our little daughter? May I hold her?'

'Not till she finish with the tit. Or else you give her the belly-ache.'

'Um. Ah, yes.' He tried again. 'What's that you're reading, my dear?'

'It is from the King – my uncle, your father.'

'So soon?'

'He hurries to congratulate us. He says to me he is delighted it is a girl.' She belched. 'But from now on I think we must work hard together to make for him a boy.'

'What?'

'But of course. The King, he says we are both young and

will have many children. He is right, yes?' Caroline wiped her lips and stared at her husband with a different sort of greed. 'I give you lots of children, so you get rid of your debts.'

He could not believe that he was hearing aright. The mere idea made a mincemeat of his thoughts and plans.

'Every baby you give me,' Caroline went raucously on, 'Parliament will give you more money for its education. Give me ten babies, and soon you owe nobody nothing. It is your only way to freedom.'

'Freedom?' he croaked.

'Let me see. I think, with luck, I will be ready to help you pay off your next portion of debts in . . . well, shall we say that we start ten days from now?'

Caroline was doubled up with glee.

He could not stay here. Not in this room with her. Could not let her see and feel what was seething up within him. Staggering away, he caught a glimpse of his own face in a pier-glass: only it was somehow not his face at all, but his father's, with eyes beginning to pop, and a vein throbbing in his temple. He rushed away, arms outstretched to push himself along between the walls of the corridor, blundering back to his bedroom. He was shouting, but did not know what his own words added up to.

Lady Jersey had gone. In any case it was not Lady Jersey he sought. The bottle . . . brandy . . . he must reach it before the attack crippled him. He was going to die, he could feel it, his mind was exploding.

He gripped the bottle, raised it.

'Trapped!' Was that his own voice yelling? 'Betrayed!'

Through the open door came two of his brothers, William and Edward. As he slumped to the floor, the Duke of Clarence stooped to get his hands under the Prince's armpits, but could not lift him. The Duke of Kent added his strength, and between them they heaved him up on to the bed.

'Don't touch me!'

The pain of being lifted and moved was excruciating. The agony, the torment, the burning – and the cramps, the closing of searing pincers on his brain . . .

'Fetch a doctor.' The Duke of Clarence waved Edward towards the door.

'No, no doctor! I can't have it. Won't. I swear I'll hurl myself from that balcony – on my skull – if you bring a . . . God, deliver me . . .'

'Is this feigned?' Edward demanded.

William was standing over his writhing older brother. He shook his head in pity and fear. 'I've suspected this once or twice. It's the same as with father.'

'Brandy, I must have brandy. Quickly.'

'George, the doctor wouldn't — '

'No doctor. You want to kill me? I know how to cure myself.' His fingers contracted, opened, groped despairingly. William reached for the brandy bottle and put it back in the Prince's hand. 'Put me in a strait-jacket and it will be the death of me. Father doesn't drink that's why he suffers. I learned the pain-killer long ago.' The Prince took a long swig and felt the scorch of the liquid driving deep down to overpower the enemy.

The Duke of Clarence sat on the edge of the bed, his arm ready to support the Prince if needed. 'How often has this happened to you?'

George was reluctant to count back and tell them. Remembering the horror of first seeing his father's madness, he had kept his own recent bouts a secret. Only Maria, in those later months with her, had known; and she, and the bottle, had been his only salvation. With her the nightmare had been kept at bay. He could even, between bouts, persuade himself that nothing serious had happened: memories faded quickly, he made no attempt to recall them or prepare for the next attack. Always there was the hope that it would not strike again. But today, under such monstrous provocation from that accursed woman, he had been seized; and now his brothers had seen for themselves.

The answer was not in being bled and purged, blistered and cupped, lashed to a chair.

'A pleasant legacy from our dear father.' He could speak now without torturing his throat. He drank again. 'Thank God there's this remedy.'

But would it always suffice? Would there come a time when the pain would overpower him, and when it was too late they would come to fetch him and lock him away?

He would die imprisoned, leaving undone so many of the things he had longed to do.

'Edward, lock the door. I have work to do.'

'But — '

'It was a mere spasm this time. But we must lay store against the future.' He got to his feet and went to the writing-desk beside the window. 'Since you have witnessed the malady, I think it as well you should witness my last will and testament.'

'George, this is no time — '

'But indeed it is the time. My life's in disorder. In chaos. I'm a ship storm-tossed on unruly seas.' He tried to grip his quill, but his fingers would not uncrook themselves at once. 'Where is the lodestar to put me back on course again? Where *is* she? How could I have let myself be trapped into this terrible situation?' He shuffled round to face the Duke of Clarence. 'How is it, brother William, that you contrive to be so content? You remain faithful to your Irish actress, and you love her, don't you? Even though she'd had four bastards by other lovers before you'd even met her.'

'I've given her three bastards more,' said William cheerfully, 'and she'll be delivering another by Christmas.'

'And you love her.'

'No other woman for me, George, ever.'

'Well said, brother William. And you, Edward – could you love any woman other than Madame de St Laurent?'

'She is the love of my life.'

'Then I too will pursue life's only satisfaction.' The

Prince's voice was growing hoarse again. 'True love: it must be, has to be.' He felt pains stabbing fitfully at him again. 'I cannot live like this. Not without my dearest Maria, not without Mrs Fitz.'

'George, you must rest.'

'Will no one bring her back to me? Maria . . .'

'The fit is returning,' said William apprehensively.

'It is not.' George steadied himself. 'Never was I more sane. Now, let us to this matter of my will.'

'Later, George.'

But later might be too late. He was insistent. Here and now his will must be written out and signed. And there would be no going back on it.

> I, George Augustus Frederick, Prince of Wales, do will, leave and bequeath all my estates and all my property of whatever kind or sort to my Maria Fitzherbert who is my wife in the eyes of God, and who is, and ever shall be, such in mine. I do also bequeath to her all money due to me from the Crown and from the Nation on the arrears of the Duchy of Cornwall.

The preparation of this and a full ten pages more was exhausting enough; but towards the end he realized that there were other questions on which he must be explicit if his wishes were not to be thwarted. He continued:

> As to my daughter, who is just born, I bequeath the whole and sole management and care of her to the King, my father, the Queen, my mother, my sisters . . . The mother of my child, called the Princess of Wales, should in no way be concerned with the education or care of the child or have possession of her person.

Of course there might be some legal quibble if he made no provision whatsoever for the bitch from Brunswick. He thought deeply, and added:

> To her who is called the Princess of Wales, I leave one shilling.
>
> Signed and willed by me, George, Prince of Wales, at Carlton House . . .

'And my wife,' he declared, 'must have a copy of this, so that she shall know I have been unfaltering in my devotion. She must see it, and know my heart – and come back to me.'

CHAPTER SIX

The Duke of Clarence, whose stout and prolific and sweetly cosseting mistress had bestowed on him so many children but never aspired to marry him, sat opposite his brother's truly married wife and said:

'I beg you, return to him.'

'No,' said Mrs Fitzherbert.

William fidgeted on his chair. This trim little, prim little villa at Acton was so cosy and so obviously designed for the suburban contentment of a middle-aged suburban couple that he could not but feel uneasy. Another man ought to have been sitting in this chair. Another man ought to have his legs sprawled out before the fire, his buttons unbuttoned, his idle chatter answered by loving inconsequences.

He ventured: 'His letters were most pitiful, didn't you think?'

'Pitiful, yes. In their dishonesty.'

'My brother is in torment.'

'I am his lawfully wedded wife,' said Mrs Fitzherbert, 'and he has disowned me.'

'On the face of it, in public, he could do no other, ma'am. The Prince is the future Defender of the English Faith.'

'And I am a practitioner of the Roman Faith?'

'For that reason the marriage has always been kept secret, as you know.'

'And secret it may remain. I have never spoken out. Never gone back on my word. But consider my position in society now – twice discarded, so that the world is encouraged to think of me merely as one of his temporary mistresses, picked up when it suits him and thrown out when it suits him.'

'The world does not think that of you, ma'am.'

'Oh, but it does. Did not Mr Fox, all that time ago, in the House of Commons tell the nation that that was all I was to him? And by going through a mockery of marriage with that Brunswick offspring was that not confirmed? One word of mine and I could have disabused them all. But I have never spoken. Others may not keep their promises. I have done so.'

The Duke said with staunch sincerity: 'I admire your loyalty, ma'am.'

'But has the Prince been loyal to me?' she flung at him. 'To me, and to my reputation? He has happily allowed it to be assumed that I am merely a disused, paid-off doxy. Not denied it, but nurtured such a slander. He — '

'Madam, pray bear with me. The truth may not be proclaimed, but it is known. The Queen herself, I believe, accepts this truth. She would wish you to be back at his side. She, my mother, the Prince's mother . . . she is concerned about George's mental state. We all fear that without you . . .'

He could find no direct way of putting it. And Mrs Fitzherbert would accept no roundabout hints and pleas and shabby evasions. She said:

'He has not merely discarded me, but allowed the circulation of discreditable lies about me. That I can never forgive.'

'And that is all you have to say to him, madam?'

'That,' said Mrs Fitzherbert, 'is all I have to say.'

The formalities could not yet be abandoned. The Princess could not be summarily banished to some far corner of the British Isles. To the Prince's fury she consulted his father and complained of being unpatriotically neglected; and when he tried to explain his detestation of her and plead for a discreet separation at the earliest possible opportunity, the King thundered that in the event of such a disgrace falling on the royal house the Prince would find himself not merely without any future increases in income but with the responsibility of surrendering much of what he already had in order to maintain his estranged wife.

So, on the face of it, the Prince and Princess of Wales remained man and wife, attending a round of boring receptions and soirées, appearing together at the races, driving through Hyde Park, and paying dutiful family visits to Windsor, where the King made an affectionate fuss of his niece, while the Queen grew colder and colder towards her. Lady Jersey, in whom the Queen had increasing confidence as a good, restraining influence on her son, continued to soothe the Prince and deride the Princess.

But the only person who could really have lifted the weight from his mind was still unresponsive.

They met, Mrs Fitzherbert and Princess Caroline, three or four times in fashionable London salons. Whereas Lady Jersey made no secret of her contempt for the Princess, Maria Fitzherbert simply bowed to her, glanced expressionlessly into the hangdog eyes of the Prince, and went her graceful way on the arm of some new, respectable escort.

The royal façade was bland enough. But Caroline began to show signs of restiveness. Two months after the birth of their child, now christened Charlotte Augusta, she introduced into a Carlton House soirée a rising young politician by the name of George Canning. She had met him at a small formal reception at Windsor, when Mr Pitt had presented him to the King as his new under-secretary for foreign affairs. He was young, eager, anxious to talk and anxious to please; and he was a Tory, and therefore all Caroline's husband most hated. She had little taste for political conversation and no clear idea of the distinction between Whig and Tory. But George hated Pitt and his entourage, and that was good enough for Caroline. She rejoiced in his fresh smile and his obvious gratitude for being adopted as her protégé.

It was unseemly to confide her personal woes in him.

But there was nobody else to whom she could talk. Her ladies-in-waiting were gossips, her Lady of the Bedchamber a scornful enemy who would twist every word she uttered and misreport it in her lover's bed. Awed by her friendship, Mr Canning was a most agreeable companion – and one with great potentialities.

'The Prince,' he observed politely as there was a clamour of argument from the alcove where some guests were playing hazard, 'looks somewhat out of sorts, ma'am.'

'And you know why? He is unwell.'

'That is how he strikes me, yes. He is — '

'*Tout à fait incapable de faire le nécessaire.*'

'He can't do the necessary?' The young man hardly dared assume she could mean what those words seemed to mean.

'No good in the bed.' Caroline rested a hand on his arm. 'Never can he give his wife what she wants. *That* is his illness.'

Canning glanced nervously to one side as the Prince came away from the gaming table, scowling, to join the Duke of Clarence.

Caroline plucked at his attention again. '*Les langues, tu sais, m'intéressent.*' The tip of her tongue dabbed slowly at her upper lip.

'Indeed, I have already been admiring your command of the French tongue.' Since something more was obviously required of him, he added: 'Have you a tutor equally fluent in the usages of the English tongue?'

Her eyes appraised him shamelessly. 'I have yet to meet someone who can teach me the English tongue in all its satisfactions.'

'If I can ever be of help, ma'am . . .'

'Thank you, Mr Canning. I think perhaps you help me in many ways.'

She looked past him, and those inviting eyes widened. He could not tell whether something had amused or alarmed her. Then came the boom of her husband's voice in his ear.

'I'm told, sir, that you are Member of Parliament for Newtown.'

'Your Royal Highness.'

Canning rose and turned to bow respectfully, and found himself subjected to the full glare of that fleshy, mottled face.

'And one of Mr Pitt's most ardent toadies.'

'I have the honour to play an active part in Mr Pitt's administration, your Royal Highness.'

'A Tory! A rip-roaring, fornicating Tory!'

'If it please your — '

'No, it does not please me. I know you not, sir. How comes it you're in my house?'

Princess Caroline said firmly: 'I invited him.'

'You?'

'With the approval of the King, your father. He does not wish me to associate with your low-bred Jacobin friends.' The Princess slid her arm through the startled Canning's. 'So I take to myself Mr George Canning. I am sure he will keep me pure in mind and body.' She bared her teeth in a snarl rather than a smile.

'Gad's 'oons,' roared the Prince, apoplectic. 'Keep me in reason.'

In answer to his plea, Lady Jersey hurried across the salon and slid her arm through his, much as Caroline had claimed her guest's.

'Come, my dear.'

The Prince of Wales stared malevolently into the gloating grin of the Princess of Wales. 'I am glad to be commanded elsewhere.' His voice was quiet now, but deadly. 'I would rather have toads and vipers crawling all over me than remain in your presence a moment longer, madam. So much you revolt me.' He pressed Lady Jersey closer as if to support himself on her fragile body. 'Come, Frances, convey me from this noxious sight. My mind cannot contain her obscenity.'

Canning had gone white, fearing at one stage that the Prince would strike him, or the Princess, or both of them. He let out a gasp of relief as the two figures moved away: the one small and fine-boned, the other gross and palpitating.

'You see?' Princess Caroline squeezed his arm. 'Even I have tried to get him drunk, at the dinner table and the breakfast table, so he do the necessary thing. But he gets drunk and still is not able. And now he makes me eat in a room alone. I am banished.'

'I can scarcely credit it.'

It was true. The Princess's coarse, animal vigour was something young Canning had never encountered before. She made him want to laugh out loud – not at her, but with her. It was incomprehensible that any man should not want to enfold this flamboyant vitality, should be capable of ignoring such frank physical generosity.

He tried to control the disorder of his thoughts. To have such thoughts about a Princess of Wales!

'My belly wishes to do its duty for the throne of England,' said Caroline, 'but how can I?'

On the first day of May in this same year, 1796, George Canning was again summoned to Carlton House. This time it was not for a formal evening but an informal private audience with the Princess. She wasted no words. Waving him to a place on the small couch beside her, where it was impossible not to brush arms and hips, she held out a letter.

'This was written by my husband yesterday. He has run away to Windsor Castle to write it. Such a man is he!'

Canning took the sheet of paper and began to read.

> Madam . . .
>
> Our inclinations are not in our power, nor should either of us be held answerable to the other, because nature has not made us suitable to each other. Tranquil and comfortable society is, however, in our power; let our intercourse, therefore, be restricted to that, and I will dis-

tinctly subscribe to the condition . . . that even in the event of any accident happening to my daughter (which I trust Providence in its mercy will avert), I shall not infringe the terms of the restriction, by proposing at any period, a connection of a more particular nature. I shall now finally close this disagreeable correspondence, trusting that, as we have completely explained ourselves to each other, the rest of our lives will be passed in uninterrupted tranquillity.

I am, Madam, with great truth,
Very sincerely yours,
George P.

Caroline was leaning over his shoulder, jabbing an indignant forefinger at lines here and there.

' "We have completely explained ourselves to each other",' she quoted shrilly. 'When has he listened to explanations from *me*?'

'Do you owe him any, ma'am?'

'No. None.'

'He says nature has not made you suitable to each other.'

Caroline's hand fell, this time not on his arm but on his leg. 'At least that is true. Never have I known a man so bad at it. And look' – she was leaning over him, her loosely confined breast brushing against him – 'here he says that even if our little baby die, he will not try to get another child by me. That is what all those words mean, is it not?'

Canning read the passage again, and had to agree that there could only be this one interpretation.

'And what is this he says? "Our inclinations are not in our power, nor should either of us be held answerable to the other." What does *that* mean, Mr Canning?'

She was still leaning across him, adjusting her weight so that it pressed him slightly backwards against the sofa. The rank smell of her armpits was strangely, indescribably exciting. The shadow between her breasts seemed deeper and more inviting as she pretended to spell out a line from her husband's letter.

Canning said breathlessly: 'I think . . . it can only mean that he gives his permission for you to do exactly as you like.'

'He does?'

She turned her face up to his, and thrust her lips moistly and greedily against his. And her fingers began to search, and tug, and torment.

CHAPTER SEVEN

Within the golden locket the exquisitely painted miniature was that of a human eye, in the minutest detail. Mrs Fitzherbert stared wonderingly into it, as she had so often lovingly, questioningly, or reproachfully stared into the original.

Edward, Duke of Kent, said: 'My brother desires you to stare at it and let it haunt you. Also there is the wording on the bracelet.'

Maria Fitzherbert turned it sceptically over between her fingers.

Rejoindre ou mourir.

She said: 'He was ever the play-actor.'

'Madam, should you see him as he is now, you would surely pity him. A death's head, that's all.'

'It is hard to picture.'

'His only diet is laudanum. Every day he demands that a pint of blood be taken from him. Constant bleeding, refusal of food . . . should he die, it must be upon your conscience, ma'am.'

'My conscience?' she said thoughtfully. 'On that score, there is only one person I can consult.'

'You will see him, then? You will — '

'I shall consult my spiritual adviser.'

'Oh. A priest?'

'Yes, a priest. I am a religious woman, your Royal Highness, and ever have been.'

Edward was about to argue, to urge some more immediate decision, and one not bounded by the religious problems which had caused so many of the couple's past troubles. But when he looked into that dignified face – a majestic face, it had to be granted – he knew there was no way of hurrying this decision.

Such was the situation as he reported it to his distraught brother.

'She can keep me waiting thus? Waiting on the decision of some Jesuit, some sly father who . . . oh, I shall not survive. Maria,' George apostrophized the wall of his Carlton House study, 'my wife, the wife of my soul, you demand my life, you shall have it, but do not keep me too long, I cannot be long for this world . . .'

His temper was not improved by the news that a decision would have to be delayed until Mrs Fitzherbert's confessor had paid a personal visit to the Pope. There were doubts whether the marriage was acceptable in the eyes of the Church. It might yet prove that the Princess of Wales was indeed, in the words of that ceremony in St James's, the Prince's lawful wedded wife. Only the Pope could pronounce. Only the Pope could assuage Mrs Fitzherbert's doubts and give her permission to return to the man who wrote of himself secretly as her husband; but showed another face and another wife to the world.

And if it were not permission but prohibition? The Prince's brothers found the prospect almost as appalling as did George himself.

Bleedings and hunger and remorse drove the Prince to declare that, whatever the judgment, he must without more ado shed all wickedness and self-indulgence. Perhaps God, seeing him do this of his own volition, would whisper the right instructions in the Pope's ear.

He summoned Lady Jersey to his study and rose to greet her with a seraphic beam.

'You look in better sorts, my darling,' she said.

'Yes, I have hope.'

'Hope for what?'

'For a better, more modest and easier life.'

She raised one fine, arched eyebrow, trying to gauge his

mood. 'You'll do as Mr Fox suggests, then, and live on half your income?'

'Indeed I will,' he vowed. 'So I may have my debts paid off in five or six years.'

'It helps now that the Princess has gone to live in Blackheath, does it not?'

He nodded eager assent. Blackheath was a comfortable distance away, Caroline could do as she chose there: take lovers if she wished them and did not create too garish a scandal, eat her onions and drink her beer.

'All things are resolved in the passage of time,' he said gravely.

'Sweetheart, I think we should decide to live quietly together at Brighton for a while, don't you?'

The Prince started. 'We?'

She reached up to touch his lapel, making a little moue which usually coaxed a kiss from him. 'The peace and sea air would do you good. I know how to work on your appetite. We shall have you your former self in no time.'

'Frances.' His manner became even more earnest. 'There is something I must tell you. It is my resolve to put all former extravagance and profligacy behind me. Depending upon the fulfilment of my most cherished hope I shall, in the future, lead a most upright and sober life.'

'Indeed you shall, my love.' Her hand reached further up, to caress his neck. 'For drink not only destroys health but impedes love's delights. We shall make love well, my dear, and you'll have no regrets in forsaking the bottle.'

'Frances, I mean also that my days of whoring are over.'

'Whoring?'

'My only hope is that God will grant I may return to my wife.'

'Your wife? But a moment ago you — '

'My true wife.'

Lady Jersey's hand fell away and she took a step back, stupefied. 'Not Mrs Fitz?'

'My only true wife,' he insisted.

The shrewd little feline face aged in a matter of seconds. The dabbing and purring and caressing could turn so soon to clawing and caterwauling. 'Are you mad? She's in the pay of the Pope, that woman, while you . . . with your father the head of the English Church, and you in good time succeeding him . . . Mad!'

'Love,' said the Prince with tears starting to his eyes, 'is all that matters in this world.'

'Ridiculous. Go back to her and you'll never have a minute's happiness.'

'We shall see.'

'You really mean that you're returning to her?'

'It all depends upon the Pope. His Holiness is deciding whether Maria and I are truly wedded or not. I await his divine ruling with impatience.'

The ruling came at last. Whether there was in it some hope of reclaiming England for the Roman Catholic faith, it was impossible to say; nor was George very interested in this or other doctrinal matters. He wanted only one answer. And the answer was that his marriage to Mrs Fitzherbert, however irregular, had divine sanction. In the eyes of God and the Church, the Prince of Wales was Maria's lawful husband. It was therefore her bounden duty to return to him.

He did not wait for her to come to him. Instead, he hastened out to her present house at Acton, a colour in his cheeks that had not been there for many a month, and paced up and down the tiny ante-room in a ferment. At the last moment it might prove all a deceit. He would be cheated yet again: after all he had done, after all his solemn resolves, he might still be betrayed.

Then a maid was holding open the door, and waiting for him within, smiling wistfully and resignedly and lovingly, was his plump and forever pleasing Maria.

'My lady, would it please you to receive His Royal Highness the Prince of Wales?'

The most glorious aspect of this glorious moment as he

swept through the door, almost knocking the maid off her feet, was the knowledge that his Maria was, truly, so pleased to received him.

On a fine day in June she gave a formal breakfast, followed by dancing. It was clear to all who attended that the Prince was back with his love. He chose the tunes the band was playing, vigorously conducted from time to time, and in between whiles paraded round Maria's garden with Maria on his arm. No further public proclamation was required: all London society knew that, once again, when the Prince was invited to a reception then Mrs Fitzherbert must be invited, and that the attendance of Mrs Fitzherbert at a soirée automatically involved the attendance of the Prince.

Caroline of Brunswick had come and gone. Things were back to normal – for a while at least.

PART THREE

FATHER AND SON

CHAPTER ONE

Early in 1801 there were signs of the King's malady recurring. His pulse quickened, his eyes rolled, his speech raced into incoherence.

'His Majesty's mind,' reported the royal physician, Dr Gisbourne, 'is in a perplexed condition.'

'Cracked,' said the Duke of York bluntly. 'Mad as a hatter, eh? Just like last time, all over again: convulsions, ravings, and strait-waistcoats.'

The Reverend Thomas Willis said: 'On that occasion my brother and I did effect a cure.'

'You'll not have the opportunity this time.' Though in his late seventies, Gisbourne had a sharp, incisive voice. He made no effort to conceal his distaste for this man, regarded by the entire profession as a charlatan.

They were gathered in the Queen's sitting-room at Buckingham House – the Duke, Willis, Gisbourne and Mr Addington, Speaker of the House – keeping their voices low in order not to distress Queen Charlotte too greatly. In fact, seated well away from them, she seemed to make no effort to follow their conversation: her mind was with her tormented husband and the horrors he would again have to endure. But Gisbourne, stung by Willis's complacency, could not let her rest. Abruptly he crossed to confront her.

'Your Majesty, I protest in the strongest terms that this man and his brother should be allowed in here at all. What right have they to physick to the King?'

'We heard the King was unwell, and something of his symptoms,' said Willis unctuously. 'My brother is in attendance on His Majesty at this moment.'

'This is outrageous, sir. Your brother's methods are a disgrace to science, and an affront to the monarchy. For a common madhouse keeper to treat the King like a mad dog, to tie him up and beat him, is scandalous.'

'Frederick,' the Queen implored her son, 'will you request this gentleman to lower his voice.'

Henry Addington pushed his stock up into his chin as if to stiffen his neck and his resolve. 'Gentlemen, in a short while I shall be Prime Minister. It is I and the Cabinet who will decide who treats the King.'

All at once they all fell silent. From the distance came a thin, wild babbling. It wailed closer, accompanied by the soft thud of running feet. The door burst open and the King blundered through in his stockinged feet, clutching his dressing-gown about him.

'Charlotte, my dear.' As the Queen hurried to his side he threw out an arm towards the Duke of York. 'My dear boy. Frederick, please, they're after me. But I can't bear to be ill again, I can't. Please. I'm well enough in my body, my heart is strong, just my head a little heated perhaps, but nothing more.' His tone rose to a screech. 'Nothing *more* – isn't that so, Gisbourne?' Then, past the physician, he saw Willis, and pressed a quavering hand to his mouth. 'Willis. What are you doing here?'

'I heard your Majesty was unwell.'

'You and your infernal brother? If I'm ill it's only because . . .' He appealed helplessly to the Duke. 'Do you know what they're trying to do to me?'

Then he swung erratically towards Addington, trying to recognize him but obviously ready to dislike him the moment he did so. Anyone connected with Parliament was in his bad books. Their misconduct had helped lead him to this. Pitt had had the impertinence to ask for a measure of Catholic Emancipation; and had resigned when the King raged at him and refused to contemplate such a monstrous breach of his Coronation oath. Addington, awaiting confirmation of his appointment as Prime Minister in Pitt's place, must tread warily if he was not further to inflame the King's burning mind.

In the doorway John Willis appeared with four brawny assistants.

'Your Majesty. Perhaps you would be good enough to return to your bedroom.'

King George's legs gave way and he crumpled into a chair.

'One moment, if you please.' Gisbourne tried to intervene.

But the Queen, pressing a lace handkerchief to her mouth, was turning resignedly away. And the Duke of York said: 'Thank you, Gisbourne, but things are worse than I feared. In the circumstances I think perhaps Dr Willis should be allowed to apply the same treatment as before.'

'I protest, your Royal Highness.'

The Duke nodded sombrely to Willis and his assistants. They stepped forward and lifted the King bodily from his chair, to take him back to the restraining chair in his bedroom, and the emetics and the beatings and the darkness, the blistering poultices and the pain which fuelled his nightmares.

Frightful agonies wracked the King's chest and stomach. His legs swelled up grotesquely. He could not bear the touch of his clothes and wig, and kept tearing them off whenever his tormentors would allow him the use of his hands.

James Harris, Lord Malmesbury, accompanied Addington to Carlton House, where the Prince of Wales and the Duke of Clarence awaited their report on the tragic turn of events.

When Harris had completed his summary, the Duke was the first to speak. 'You would say, then, that my father's incapable of the business of government?'

'Certainly.'

William silently consulted his brother.

'It's a hard blow to bear,' said the Prince levelly. 'Thank you, Harris.' When the Earl of Malmesbury had left, he turned to Addington. 'What do you think, hey? What do we do?'

'Sir?'

'The country can't do without a Head of State. No one to give the Royal Assent. Government will grind to a halt.'

'Tragic, sir.'

The Prince wondered how one was to get anything through to this stolid, incredibly obtuse man.

The Duke of Clarence came to his rescue. 'Oughtn't we to look at the 1788 Regency Bill again? Bring it up to date, eh, in case it has to be put into operation?'

'Mr Pitt is still nominally Prime Minister, sir,' Addington hedged. 'Ought you not to ask him?'

'Oh, damn Pitt,' said the Prince. 'You'll be Prime Minister in a week or so.'

'But I'm not so yet.' Addington could not conceal his relief. There were compensations for having to defer fulfilment of his ambition.

Pitt was summoned. But the Prince of Wales was not going to deal with his old enemy unsupported. He insisted on Fox being present at the meeting.

Neither man looked at his best. Pitt tried to maintain his characteristic cold aloofness, but from tiredness and overwork was subject to little tremors and tics almost as distressing as the King's. Fox, excluded from office for so many years and with so few signs of ever being able to return until the Prince of Wales came to power, had lost some of his old panache, and was beginning to show the swellings and heaviness of dropsy.

But Pitt was consistent in one thing. Thirteen years had gone by, and still he was inflexible: 'The Regency Act is for a restricted Regency, your Royal Highness. You are debarred from dissolving Parliament and forming a new government of your choice.'

Fox's glum, sagging jowls sank even further. 'Either the King's mad, or he's not. If he is, it's the same thing constitutionally as if he were dead.'

'I disagree.'

'Someone,' said the Prince, 'has got to be Head of State.'

'Your father still is, sir. And the Willises assure me that in good time — '

'The Willises want only to make money. It's said that when they examine their own tongues in the mirror each morning they pass a guinea from one waistcoat pocket to the other.'

'And at the moment,' said Fox bitterly, '*they* are governing the country, Mr Pitt. Make no mistake about that.'

Pitt looked uneasy. Addington was soon to be infected with that unease. When papers were taken to Buckingham House for signature, he was not allowed into the royal presence. The Reverend Thomas Willis insisted that places for signature should be marked with a cross; and in due course he returned with the papers duly signed. When there were longer delays than usual, Addington suspected the King's keepers were using coercion or the threat of the straight-jacket; but provided he could carry a clear royal signature away with him, the work of the country could go on and he preferred not to ask too many distressing questions.

He worried most when he did not carry away such a warrant. Every now and then the Willises decided that a certain measure might distress the King, and then took it on themselves to return it disapprovingly to the Parliamentary emissary.

In spite of these compromises, the administration did in fact begin to slow down. Addington could not formally take office because Pitt could not formally surrender the seals of office. But Pitt could not and would not continue as Prime Minister unless he were given his way over Catholic Emancipation: and that was a subject never to be breathed in the King's presence, in either his mad moments or sane moments.

It was the Duke of York who took decisive action. With his mother at his side he announced that he would be kept from his father no longer. He must see him and talk with him, and assess the truth for himself. The Willises protested. A visit would upset His Majesty; given a few days there might be an improvement; but there must be no immediate excitement.

'What have you done to him?' demanded the Duke.

'Done, sir? Why, done our best, as ever.'

'Come, mother.'

John Willis blundered agitatedly after the Queen and the Duke as they marched regally towards the King's suite.

In the bedroom, the King lay strapped to his bed. His eyes, though terrified, were clear. He stared imploringly at his wife and son.

'Charlotte, look what they are doing to me. I was coming to visit you this morning, and they would not permit it. But I am well. See for yourself how well I would be if only I were free from this torture.'

The Queen hesitated; then hurried to him and began to fumble, sobbing, with the straps.

'Our only concern,' Thomas Willis hastened to say, 'has always been with His Majesty's well-being.'

'Really?' The Duke was advancing threateningly on him.

'If your Royal Highness thinks there is scope for a variation in the treatment — '

'There is scope for a variation in the doctors,' said the Duke. 'I think we shall prefer Dr Gisbourne to resume treatment.'

'If I may offer a few words of advice, sir — '

'You may not. My father is hereby removed from your charge. And he will be taken away from this place and into the country, to recover from your *treatment*.'

The choice of a country retreat offered few problems. Windsor was too large, too formal, and too much associated with political duties and ceremonials. The little palace at Kew was still the King's favourite.

It was at Kew, a few weeks later, that his eldest son walked with him: the King setting a slow, steady pace, the

Prince of Wales lumbering and puffing but endeavouring to look as if he enjoyed every moment of it.

'Of course,' said the King, 'I realize my recovery has come as a bitter blow to you.'

'Father, no, really!'

'To you and all your Whig cronies. Just waiting to cringe to the French, give away all we have fought so hard for, encourage assassinations and revolutions. Pah! Fox and Sheridan tried to visit me, y'know. I daresay to see how much longer they'd have to wait.'

'None of us thought for one moment — '

'No? What about the Morning Chronicle, then, announcing my death and publishing a list of *your* new ministers, with Fox at the top? Eh?'

The Prince stared down at the grass, mortified. 'A dreadful mistake. Can't imagine how it happened.'

'Well, it's over and I'm almost well again.' They trod on in silence for a while. The smell of newly scythed grass was sweet, and somewhere in an invisible height a lark was singing deliriously. 'You know, George,' said the King, 'you and I ought not to be forever arguing over everything. What, what? D'you know, when I really thought death was upon me, it was our breach, our dislike of each other that troubled me more than anything else.'

The Prince came to a standstill; and burst into tears.

'Good heavens.' His father was aghast. 'Here, dry your eyes. Stand still.' He pulled out a crumpled handkerchief and dabbed at the Prince's eyes. 'Calm down, do. Here, take my arm.'

The Prince did so. 'I'm so sorry. It's awful to be always fighting.' He gulped.

'We must be better friends in future, heh?'

'Father, I do hope so.'

They walked on. Then the King, after a few bars of humming one of his favourite themes from Handel's *Esther*, came out with it: 'And now you'll go and see Caroline at Blackheath and be reconciled with her too, won't you?'

The Prince's heart sank. 'Oh, father!'

'Terminate your connection with that Fitzherbert woman. Show me you're in earnest. Back to your wife, boy.'

'But I hate the sight of her. And the smell of her. And it must be bedlam down there. They tell me she's filled the place with children, God knows whose — '

'Your own among them.'

'Only on visits. As we agreed. I wouldn't let Charlotte out of my sight long enough for her to be tainted.'

'She's hardly ever *in* your sight.' The King's temper and countenance grew hectic again. 'Left with only nursery-maids to play with at Carlton House while you gallivant off to Brighton, or spend your nights with that Fitzherbert creature.'

'Charlotte loves Carlton House. Plays in the garden by the hour.'

'It's time her education was seriously commenced. I shall want to know what you have in mind. And I shall want to know you've discussed the matter with the Princess of Wales.'

'If I did ever go to see her,' said his son gloomily, 'I'd need to borrow your strait-jacket on my return.'

The tell-tale vein in the King's temple began to beat ominously. But as they approached the Prince's coach by the Dutch House he said in a warmly appealing tone: 'Let's be sure we're better friends in future, hey, my boy?'

George thought of the beatings, the contemptuous remarks, the awful clothes and the awful disappointments. But he took his father's hand and nodded and smiled, and wiped away one last suspicion of a tear. Only when he was in his coach on the way back to London did he stretch out, undo a few buttons, and allow himself the unfilial thought: Pompous old ass.

They had been clattering along for a good half-hour when there was the brisk trot of hoofs behind, followed by a pistol shot in the air. Instinctively George ducked; then puffed indignantly round to lean out of the window.

His brother Edward came cantering up alongside.

'George, those damned quacks have him again.'

'What?'

'The Willises. They've taken physical charge of him. Virtually kidnapped him.'

The coach slowed. The Duke of Kent reined in his panting chestnut.

'But I left him not much more than thirty minutes ago,' protested the Prince. 'He was in good enough spirits then. What happened?'

'He said something angry. Nothing more than usual, but his manner alarmed mother, and she allowed the Willises to have their way. They must have been biding their time, staying close – and hoping. Now they've got him, and father was already starting to rave again as I left.'

The Prince of Wales trembled. He fought down his own fright. But somehow he seemed to feel the bonds, the scorch of the poultices, the creeping visions . . .

'Get in.' He leaned further out to shout up to his coachman. 'Back to Kew Palace, and bring the Duke's horse behind. Quick, now!'

As Edward settled into the opposite seat he said: 'It was dreadful. I couldn't get back into the house, they wouldn't let me, but I could hear him raving.'

'So.' The Prince sank back against the creaking leather. 'So a Parliamentary Enquiry could still happen.'

'Eh? Oh, I suppose so, yes.'

George pondered a moment, then tapped the roof of the coach. 'Coachman? Not Kew. London.' He heaved himself into a more comfortable position. 'We really have no business to interfere with the course of medical science.'

CHAPTER TWO

The King said: 'No, Mr Willis, I will not sign this decree.'

'Your Majesty, I was hoping we could be spared further unpleasantness.'

'I insist on seeing Addington himself.'

'I cannot allow that.'

'I haven't seen a Christian face since heaven knows when,' said the King firmly. 'Let my Prime Minister be brought to me. Bring him out here now, this minute, sir.'

Willis began to edge shiftily round him towards the terrace, as if to block the way from the casement windows. But at that moment Addington stepped out into the garden.

'Forgive me, your Majesty.'

'My dear fellow, it's good to see you. I appeal to you. You see me in good health, do you not, but I cannot perform any function, cannot go anywhere but there's one of these creatures watching for an excuse to persecute me. I must be released. At once.'

Addington glanced warily at Willis. 'I'll raise the matter in Cabinet, sir.'

'No. I mean today. Now.'

'Well, sir. Hm, yes. But could we attend first to this document?' He nodded at the paper Willis was still holding. 'It really is imperative that you should sign it. It's the War Office Act, and until your Majesty gives your assent . . .'

The King, apparently subdued, was reaching for the paper. The moment it was in his hands he methodically tore it in two and then in two again.

'I absolutely refuse,' he said with regal magnificence, 'to sign any paper whatsoever until I am released. I have heard of men withholding their labour or professional services when they have cause for dissatisfaction — '

'There are dangerous movements afoot, your Majesty, it is true.'

'Then I shall start one of my own. I hereby make a solemn declaration that unless these wretches are thrown out bag and baggage and I am allowed to live where and how I choose, no earthly consideration shall induce me to sign my name to any paper or authorize one act of government whatsoever. Do I make myself clear?'

CHAPTER THREE

Church bells were pealing up the slope from Greenwich and along the ridge of Blackheath. At intervals they were drowned by peals of uncontrollable laughter as the Princess of Wales urged her six-year-old daughter to down a large mug of beer in honour of the King.

'But it's horrid,' Charlotte spluttered. 'I don't want it.'

'You must drink to grandpapa's health, darling.'

'I won't.'

Caroline took a long puff at her black cigar. 'My pet, your grandfather has been very good to us. He loves you, he looks after me. And now that he is better, it's only right you should be like his other loyal subjects.'

'Will father be drinking the King's health?'

George Canning, perched on the arm of the sofa, snorted a laugh. The little Princess looked at him quizzically, then without warning tipped back the mug and drank her beer. For a moment it looked likely that she would sick it all up again. Then she tightened her lips, took a deep breath, and shrieked.

'All right, then,' said her mother indulgently. 'Run along, then. I shall tell grandpa you wished him well.' She waited until the door was firmly closed, then edged closer to Canning. 'Sometimes I think the King is the only true friend I have in this horrible country.'

His hand drooped over the back of the sofa and prodded the back of her neck. 'There's me.'

'You're no friend.'

His fingers stroked, tightened. 'That's not what you said last night.'

'That's different. Nothing to do with friendship.' She tilted her head back to grin at him. 'But I like it.'

'Good.' He slid down towards her.

'No one at all likes me, just for myself.' Caroline sighed, and reached for solace in the form of a Spanish onion from a regularly emptied bowl. She pulled up her skirts and prodded Canning's shin experimentally with her foot. 'Do you know what my pig of a husband has done now? Cut my allowance in half. One half! If it were not for the King, making me Ranger of Greenwich Park and moving me into this nice house, I'd have been destitute these last three years and more.'

Four or five children went screaming happily past the window, and there were sounds of a cheerful scuffle breaking out somewhere in the shrubbery. Canning, worried lest one of them should stare in and see the Princess wriggling closer and more suggestively towards him, got up and went to look out over the garden.

'And do you know what else?' Caroline went on. 'My Caroline, my own darling daughter, he negotiates to forbid me any access to her. Trying to get the King on his side by promising the King can share her, have her down at Windsor.'

'Perhaps,' Canning hazarded, 'he feels that all these children here, and this carefree way of life, are a bad influence on her.'

Caroline crunched savagely into another onion. 'And what about the influences at Carlton House? What about the influence of all his whores, and that fat old whore Fitzherbert?'

'I believe she's his *only* whore at the moment.'

'Ha! Him, he has the roving eye, and where the eye roves, other parts of him are not long following.'

Canning summoned up the courage to turn and face her with what he hoped appeared a statesmanlike gravity.

'I should warn you: the more stories that come out of this house, the weaker your position. You lack discretion, my dear. The wildest rumours are flying around London about what happens down here. Who spreads these tales?'

'What do I care? It is good, it is what I want for the pig.'

'But don't you see, if you give him too much he'll have grounds for a full legal separation, and for keeping Charlotte to himself. At worst there could be a divorce.'

'He could not divorce me.'

'He wouldn't hesitate. And others could suffer.' This was an awkward moment. He had lain awake worrying about it, wondering how to put the matter to her without bringing a shower of colourful abuse down about his head. 'He would wish to involve as many people as possible. And it's high treason to commit adultery with the wife of an heir to the throne.'

'So that is it? You think just of yourself.'

'No, I assure you. Mostly of you.'

'What do I care?' she said again, swinging her legs from the sofa so that for a second Canning thought she was about to leap at him and give battle. 'I am having happiness here, with these children. I like children in my house, and I shall have more when it pleases me.'

Canning glanced over his shoulder at the eruption of grubby, yelling children from an arbour. 'You have six here already,' he pointed out.

'For Charlotte to play with when she comes.'

'The story is that they're most of them yours.'

Caroline hooted with laughter. 'That is good. Especially as I *am* going to have another myself.'

Canning stared in mounting terror as she slowly turned her profile before him and patted her stomach.

'Had you not noticed, darling?' she continued. 'Look. See. Do you want a brother or a sister for your other child?'

'You mean . . . you really mean we . . .'

'I'm glad you show such delight. In fact I am not having a baby. It is just that I put on weight.' As he went past her in search of his tumbler of gin, she blew cigar smoke in his face. 'Ha, I fright you? You look so funny. That is the sort of shock I would like to give the pig. When I am Queen, *then* let him watch out.'

The noise of the children receded and then returned. Suddenly they came tumbling in from outdoors, two little ones going down on all fours on the stained carpet, while the others skipped round in what appeared to be some strange ritual dance. It was only as they whooped away across the room that Canning saw a wriggling white shape in the heart of the hullabaloo. They had driven a tame rabbit in from the garden and were trying to corner it. All at once the youngest child, two-year-old Willy Austin, made a plunge, grabbed the animal, and went rushing off into the passage with the rest in hot pursuit.

Caroline clapped her hands. 'Did you see little Willikin? He's getting such a bright little boy, don't you think?'

Canning preferred to keep his opinions on Willikin to himself. There had already been much speculation about this particular child. Caroline had presented the infant to her visitors almost two years ago without warning, when he was a mewling, skinny little thing, and declared she had adopted him from a docker's family. She cared for the boy herself, kept him in her bedroom, spoiled him, let him throw food about at table and paw Mr Pitt or Lady Hester Stanhope with sticky fingers; and was forever lavishing praise on his beauty, his intelligence, his winning ways. Canning was saved from having to make some fulsome comment by the arrival in the doorway of a tight-lipped woman in her early forties, her sarsenet pelisse tugged awry as if she had just encountered the infant charge head-on.

'Charlotte!' said the Princess heartily. 'Did you see little Willikin with the rabbit?'

'I did, your Royal Highness,' said Lady Douglas. 'You are so much in your element with children, are you not?'

Canning heard, if Caroline did not, the acid stab beneath the precise little voice. Charlotte Douglas he knew to be a bitch, and a trouble-making bitch at that. It crossed his mind that a lot of the gossip emanating from this house could have been carried by this supposedly friendly neighbour.

'Do you know,' Caroline chattered, taking her visitor's arm and drawing her into the room, 'that Lady Oxford has a nursery of eight children, and they're all really her own, by the gardening staff?'

'Ma'am, I came to inform you that — '

'It's true, it's true, her laundrywoman told mine.'

'Always wanted to be a gardener,' Canning insinuated.

'George!' Caroline elbowed him in the ribs as she passed.

Charlotte Douglas said: 'Your Royal Highness, you must listen. I came to tell you that the King is on his way.'

'The King? But — '

'He will be here any moment. I saw him from some distance and felt I ought to forewarn you.'

To warn her, mused Canning, or gloatingly to witness the encounter?

'Quickly!' cried the Princess. 'Pull those cushions straight – that table, over there in the corner – and, oh dear, someone has spilt . . . I must wash Willikin, and find Charlotte, and . . .'

The King rode in at the garden gate, swung nimbly from the saddle, and tugged at the wide lapels of his bright blue riding-coat as he strode into the house with a breezy, expectant smile.

'Your Majesty.'

Lady Douglas had at some time practised her Court bow to perfection.

'No ceremony, no ceremony.' The King drew Caroline to him and kissed her. When he stood back he extended a friendly hand towards Canning, then towards Lady Douglas.

'This is such a surprise,' fluttered the Princess. 'If I had known, I would have had Charlotte waiting for you.'

'Sorry to interrupt. Felt I'd like to see my granddaughter

while she's down here, eh, what-what? And you m'dear, of course.'

'And some of the other children would be most honoured to meet you, your Majesty. Little Willy Austin is a special treasure.'

'Don't know him. Never heard of him.'

'I'm sure I told you I'd adopted him.'

Voices streamed away under the window again. The King glanced idly out. Caroline came to his side and pointed eagerly. 'Over there, by the pond.'

'Adopted, did you say?'

'And we know all about that, don't we?' said Lady Douglas to Canning in what purported to be an undertone, but which he knew had been pitched to reach the royal ear.

King George stiffened. Caroline, unconscious of danger, was still smiling and pointing; but the King's attention was all on Lady Douglas.

'What did you say, madam?'

'Your Majesty?'

'You made a remark to your companion. Pray what was it?'

Canning ventured: 'Just what a delightful child this —'

'I was not addressing you, sir.'

'A lovely boy.' Lady Douglas was shaken, but quick to recover. 'Fine face. He even *looks*,' she said sweetly, 'like the Princess of Wales.'

Much less affable than when he arrived, the King returned his gaze to the little group about the pond.

'How often does this boy visit you, then?'

'He lives here,' said Caroline.

The King's hand began to tremble. He willed it to remain steady by glaring at it, unblinking. At last he said: 'I must see little Charlotte. I'll go out and find her.'

'I'll summon her in a few minutes, sir, when I've —'

'I shall see her outside.'

The King left a marked chill in the room. Lady Douglas backed away from Canning's accusing frown; and even the

Princess belatedly realized that something had gone wrong.

'If you will excuse me . . .' Lady Douglas made for the door.

As she left, Canning said: 'That meddlesome woman! Do you understand the suspicion she has put into the King's mind?'

'About what?'

'About your precious Willikin. Whose face is so like yours.'

'He thinks that Willy is mine?' The Princess forced a laugh. 'Well, let him believe what he likes.' She grew more sober. 'No, that might be troublesome. If he does think it — '

'You can always say your husband is the father.'

Caroline was struck with a genuine fit of laughter, but controlled it as she went to the window. The King had reached the pond and was looking down into the awed, upturned faces of the children. He put his hand on a shoulder, and drew little Willikin from the group. He was peering intently, very intently, into the boy's face.

Caroline said fretfully: 'They say the whore Fitzherbert is scheming to adopt a child. And whose child will *that* claim to be?' Anxiously she watched Willikin and the King. 'And why should she be able to do as she chooses, while I am suspected and persecuted?'

CHAPTER FOUR

There were two empty seats at the Prince's table. The scene was dazzling, but George's brow was dark. Candles winked in the facets of crystal goblets, and beads of light fell from the great chandeliers to dance and spark in the silver finger-bowls. Light flashed, too, whenever the Prince moved in his chair: his full hussar uniform, designed by himself, was embellished with clusters of diamonds which glinted every time he took in breath or a mouthful of pheasant. To one side of him sat Maria Fitzherbert, a strand of hair damp across her forehead, and eyes pink with weeping; on his other hand was the statuesque Lady Hertford, her hair piled high as if to reach the chandeliers, with not a wisp out of place. But the Prince took no pleasure in the company. Time and again he glowered at the empty places.

Framed between a great vase of roses and a branched epergne filled with fruit, James Harris shook his head regretfully. 'I'm afraid there's no doubt that the Seymour executors are prepared to oppose Mrs Fitzherbert's guardianship of little Minnie with the utmost purpose.'

'But I have cared for the child almost since her birth,' said Maria wretchedly.

'We are all aware of that, ma'am.'

'A cruel situation,' said Lady Hertford quietly.

'I entirely agree,' said Harris.

They all awaited the Prince of Wales's reaction. He had in fact paid scant attention, and was once again moodily contemplating the vacant seats.

'Dearest.' Maria beseeched his attention.

'Mm?'

'Lord Malmesbury has been telling us how things stand with Minnie.'

'I was saying, sir, that the adoption of — '

'Yes, yes, Harris,' said the Prince tetchily. 'Fox and Sheridan are taking a devilish long time.'

'I'm sure they would start from Westminster the moment the military debate ended. And there can be no doubt of the outcome. It would be unthinkable for you not to receive the recognition you merit at this grave moment in our country's history.'

Maria said: 'Dearest, about Minnie — '

'All the truest elements in the country are behind you, sir,' said Lady Hertford.

The rich resonance, the aristocratic assurance, of her voice calmed the Prince. He offered her a grateful smile. She was one of those superb, accomplished, confident women whose approval could not but give a man confidence also, just when he most needed it.

Mollified, he turned back to Maria, though her weeping struck him as excessive. And the subject was hardly a suitable one for an evening such as this, when there was so much else at stake.

'I beg your pardon.' He forced himself to be attentive. 'Harris, the adoption?'

It had to be admitted that he himself was the one who from the start had most fervently advocated Maria's taking charge of the little Seymour girl. She was such a ravishing child, and so much like her mother. The Prince had passed some happy hours with Maria's old friend, Lady Horatia Seymour, during that aimless period before Maria came back to him. Her husband had been much out of England in naval service, and when Lady Horatia's baby Mary was born he had been on the high seas for quite some time. A few spiteful tongues prattled of dates which did not fit certain calculations.

In Lady Horatia's own absence, seeking a cure for a number of ailments, the Prince of Wales had persuaded his homecoming Maria to care for the child. Now that both Lady Horatia and her husband were dead, Mary – always Minnie to her friends – was still in Mrs Fitzherbert's care, and Maria had asked, on her own husband's insistence, that she might now formally adopt her.

But Harris was explaining: 'The executors oppose Mrs Fitzherbert's guardianship on the grounds of her Catholic faith, sir.'

'Monstrous,' whispered Maria.

Lady Hertford said: 'My husband and I are not of Mrs Fitzherbert's faith, but as members of the Seymour family ourselves we would not for a moment cast any slur on her treatment of the girl.'

'Thank you,' said the Prince. 'Maria is terribly upset. It's good of you.'

He was aware from the corner of his eye that Maria, as if detecting something in his manner, had stopped dabbing at her tears and was studying him intently.

'I have an idea,' said Lady Hertford.

Maria leaned forward to look, hopeful yet perturbed, across the swelling expanse of her husband's beribboned and bejewelled stomach.

'As we have mentioned,' Lady Hertford went on, tilting her patrician nose in the air and adjusting her swansdown tippet to allow the Prince a radiant vision of her bosom and magnificent shoulders, 'my husband and I are closely related to the family concerned. Poor dear Hugh was my husband's brother. If *we* are prepared to entrust our niece to Mrs Fitzherbert, who will dare to frown?'

Harris said: 'My Lady, this is a generous gesture. But the fact remains that the House of Lords has already turned down the case brought by His Royal Highness on Mrs Fitzherbert's behalf against the executors.'

'Who have still found no one else to act as guardian.' Lady Hertford caught the Prince's appreciative eye, and nodded with reassuring conviction. 'One of the executors is another of the family. I shall speak to my husband. I fancy it would be difficult for anyone to contest the suitability of Lord Hertford and myself as the child's guardians.'

'Most assurely not, ma'am. But I fail to see — '

'As her legal guardians,' said Lady Hertford smoothly, 'we would have every right to ask whomsoever we chose to act on our behalf in sheltering and bringing up the child.'

The Prince dropped his fork and stared at her with ever-increasing admiration. Such a radiant mind, in such a superb body!

'You would leave her where she is?'

'We would appoint Mrs Fitzherbert to care for Minnie. which means, as your Royal Highness so shrewdly observes, that she would be left where she is.'

Maria let out a sob of joy and put her hand on the Prince's sleeve. But he was still looking full at his neighbour on the other side.

'Lady Hertford, if I may be permitted, that's brilliant.'

He was rewarded with a gracious, intoxicating smile.

With that weight off his mind, the Prince returned to his food, only to be disconcerted yet again by the sight of those still unfilled places. One worry had been disposed of, only to make way for a worse one.

He could barely contain himself when at last the dining-room doors opened to admit a footman announcing Mr Fox and Mr Sheridan.

The Prince was on his feet. 'Well?'

'Nothing,' said Fox.

'You can't mean — '

'The vote went against us,' said Sheridan.

The Prince raised his glass and hurled it to the floor. Splinters spurted out in a brief fountain.

'God damn and blast the whole foul lot of them! Am I to go mad with inactivity?'

Harris nodded the newcomers towards their waiting chairs; but Fox and Sheridan, glancing at the Prince's empurpled face, deemed it more tactful not to sit down until the tension had eased.

It showed no sign of doing so. The story of failure could not be diluted or allowed to simmer down. The Prince's expectations had been unreasonably high this time. They were to be unreasonably abased.

With the uneasy truce with France ended, and the growing menace of the upstart but brilliant Napoleon Bonaparte casting covetous eyes on the shores of England, military preparations were going ahead again with redoubled vigour. Local militia drilled, defences were hastily conceived along the south coast, officers looked forward eagerly to promotion, battle, glory, and further promotion. Still the Prince of Wales had no more than an honorary colonelcy in the Dragoons. How could he be regarded by his countrymen as anything but a laughing stock? He had written repeatedly to the King; and been told not to mention the matter again. He had taken Addington aside and harangued him by the hour; and Addington reported that he had spoken to the King and received a most unpromising reply. The effort of the Prince's Whig friends in Parliament was a last fling: and even then the public would know nothing of his eagerness to set a good, gallant example, since the Strangers' Gallery had been cleared before the debate and there would be no published report.

Fox pleaded. Why should the services of the heir to the throne be so spurned? He was in the prime of life and capable of the utmost energy. The whole country demanded to know why he was not granted higher rank and a seat on the General Council being formed to prosecute the war.

The Tories knew whose side it was safer to be on. They voted down the Prince's friends.

Of his younger brothers, the Duke of York was confirmed as Commander-in-Chief; the Duke of Clarence was promoted to the rank of Admiral; and the Dukes of Kent and Cumberland were made Major-Generals.

Stricken silence fell on the Prince's dinner table.

'Dearest,' Maria ventured, 'you know your family has

always had a tradition of denying office to the heir because — '

'Hold your tongue.' He did not even deign to look at her, but pounded the table and shouted at Fox and Sheridan: 'You failed me!'

'Sir, we — '

'I regret that dinner is concluded.'

Fox and Sheridan stood rigid for a moment, then made curt bows and turned towards the door.

Mrs Fitzherbert protested: 'Dearest — '

'I have already requested you to hold your tongue.' The Prince waited until Fox and Sheridan had departed, then collapsed disconsolately into his chair. After a couple of minutes he managed a bleak smile in Lady Hertford's direction. 'I don't suppose you have a ready solution for *this*?'

'Not immediately, sir.' She pursed her lips, and if she was still smiling it was reflectively, to herself alone. 'But usually there are ways of achieving a desired object, somehow, whatever it may be.'

The Prince leaned closer. 'Lady Hertford. Isabella. If you can help me in this . . .'

'Sir,' said Maria, behind him.

He ignored her. He and Lady Hertford had settled the question of the girl Minnie in her favour; now it was surely his turn to have his own wishes gratified. Lady Hertford would know how. High Tory she might be, but he suspected she might have more to offer than the Whigs he had so loyally backed and who had now so resoundingly let him down.

CHAPTER FIVE

The King was blind. It had come upon him without warning. Although he had often been shaken by tremors which hinted at worse things to come, his old plague had not fully returned to seize him. During previous bouts he had sometimes been blinded by pain or made dizzy in a raging fever. This was different. He simply awoke one morning to find that he could not see.

So now he must have all his correspondence read over to him, dictate his answers, and have his hand guided to the place where his signature must be scrawled on official documents.

It was embarrassing for some of those who read to him. Lord Malesbury found himself once more in the position of a diplomatic purveyor of dubious news; but this time could not tactfully interpret it. The King had heard a whisper of something scurrilous in the newspapers. His Prime Minister had let slip one hint and then tried to retract it. What were they all hiding from him? Harris was the only man he had learned to trust. Harris must read to him; and read the truth.

Clearing his throat, Harris committed himself to yet another unrewarding task.

'Did your Majesty at any time receive from His Royal Highness the Prince of Wales a letter asking that he should be allowed to display the best energies of his character and to shed the last drop of his blood in support of your Majesty's person, Crown, and dignity?'

'Eh? What-what? Of course I did. Just the sort of thing he's always writing, dammit.'

'And were you aware that His Royal Highness submitted through Mr Addington a request that he might – um – "set an example to excite the loyal energies of the nation"?'

'Sounds just like George, yes.' The King groped through the unhappy fog of his affliction. 'But you're not telling me he's been spreading these absurdities before the public? He knows my answers well enough.'

Harris folded over a column of the Morning Chronicle. With plodding fatalism he asked: 'Did you on one occasion answer His Royal Highness's submissions by declaring, "I am aware that extensive promotion has taken place in the Army. I am aware also that your brothers have all received high command. Nevertheless, considering the repeated declarations I have made upon this matter I had flattered myself to have heard no further from you. I absolutely and utterly refuse to give you any employment, military or civilian, and if you trouble me on this matter once more, may you be utterly damned. Your affectionate father, George R." Did you write anything of this kind, your Majesty?'

'That he should have the discourtesy to publish this! The impertinence! Our private and personal letters . . .'

'So they are true?'

'Not for public consumption, sir.'

'The public, your Majesty,' Harris regretted, 'will be avidly consuming them.'

'Who put him up to this? What does he hope to gain?'

Harris could have answered both questions, but felt that diplomatic silence was more appropriate. The bewildered, blundering King claimed to want the truth but in truth had no appetite for truth. In his present sad temper he wanted only a butt for his anger. That his son should, in the hope of public sympathy, publicly reveal what had passed between them, and at the same time by innuendo and disobedience slander and spit upon the Princess of Wales, flout his father's wishes for a reconciliation, and continue treacherously to consort with the Whigs who still debated the chances of peace with France, was a canker more painful than all his other ailments. Whatever in this world went wrong, from Paris to the Brighton Pavilion, was the Prince of Wales's fault.

Not that he had not had his own doubts about certain aspects of the Princess of Wales's conduct. But if the Prince had behaved properly to her in the first place, and asserted his authority as well as showing affection, such doubts would never have arisen.

Unfortunately for the King, there was a further shock in store.

Awakening belatedly to the source of many discreditable stories about her, Princess Caroline had written Lady Douglas a curt note breaking off all relationships between them. Stung to an angry response, Sir John and Lady Douglas got in touch with the Duke of Sussex and told him every unsavoury episode they could recall at Blackheath. They were pressed to make a sworn statement, which Lady Douglas dictated with some relish; and this had to be read out to the King.

Harris demurred, and found an excuse for dodging the task. It was left to the Duke of Clarence to break the bad news to his father.

Lady Douglas testified that in the autumn of the year 1801, when she first made the acquaintance of her neighbour at Blackheath, the Princess had told her she was with child, and had been these four months.

> Upon my return to Blackheath in February, I called upon Her Royal Highness and found her packing a small black box, and an infant sleeping on the sofa, with a piece of scarlet cloth thrown over it. She appeared confused, and hesitated whether she should be rude or kind, but recovering herself, chose to be the latter. Upon my remarking on the child, Her Royal Highness said, "Here is the little boy. I bore him last month, though upon my life I don't know which of them is the father. I am thinking of calling him William Austin."

She went on to explain that Willikin usually slept in the Princess's own bedroom, when it was not shared with others: for in addition to the evidence regarding the boy, Lady Douglas added that the Princess had boasted of having intimate relations with Admiral Sir Sydney Smith, a Captain Manby, and Sir Thomas Lawrence, the portrait painter who had depicted her in such a flattering light.

When the Duke of Clarence had reached the end of the testimony, his father lay utterly still, his head back against the pillows, his body stretched limp and almost lifeless along the bed. Sightless eyes were raised in what might have been a desperate prayer. At last he spoke.

'Is my Prime Minister in attendance?'

'Yes, father.'

'Ask Mr Pitt to step this way, then.'

'Father, Mr Pitt died in January,' said the Duke gently. 'The Prime Minister now is Lord Grenville.'

'Well, ask him to come in.'

The Duke fetched Lord Grenville who, as leader of a coalition government dubbed the Ministry of All the Talents, had learned to be circumspect and calculating in all things; preserved an impassive countenance and face, preferring never to commit himself until a positive lead had been given, never to initiate a conversation which might betray his personal motives; and today felt nothing but distaste for the subject which the Duke of Clarence had hinted would have to be dicussed.

'Your Majesty.'

'Lord . . . er . . .' The King drew a hand across his eyes, then let it flop back to his side. 'Mr Prime Minister. I have this day received a document containing allegations against the Princess of Wales of such a nature that, if they are true, show my judgment of humankind through the forty-six years of my reign to have been at fault.' His voice grew sterner. 'I instruct you to set up a commission to investigate them. Yourself, and of course the Lord Chancellor, Lord . . . er . . .'

'Erskine,' Grenville supplied coldly.

'Erskine, yes. And the Chief Justice . . .'

'Lord Ellenborough.'

'Just so. You will hold an investigation into the alleged adultery of Princess Caroline, and the parentage of the infant William Austin. Give him the statement, William.' When he had heard the rustle of the document being passed over, the King concluded: 'You will act discreetly. A *delicate* investigation, if you please, Mr Pitt.'

Grenville bowed and left. The Duke of Clarence hesitated, then pulled a rug up to his father's neck, kissed his brow, and followed the Prime Minister.

The King wept.

CHAPTER SIX

Often the Prince of Wales had waited for news, good or bad, at his pavilion in Brighton. There he had been when a great British Victory at Trafalgar was announced, though accompanied by the terrible news of Lord Nelson's death. There he and his friends, on the first rumours of a defeat at Austerlitz, had believed the defeat to have been that of Napoleon; and there they had, all too soon, heard that the truth was quite the reverse. In the repeatedly redecorated rooms, many of them assuming more and more of a Chinese character as time went on, the Prince had impatiently awaited more than one lady who had taken his fancy. He was at Brighton when news of his father's intention to instigate the Delicate Investigation was confirmed. And Brighton was, at such times, a pleasanter place to be than London. Whatever they might privately think of him, the local tradesmen were invariably civil: his presence did, after all, guarantee them such an increase of fashionable custom. In London he was rarely safe from abuse and malice. Publication of his correspondence with his father over military matters had made him less rather than more popular. And the Delicate Investigation, dragging on with the taking of evidence from servants and anyone with a tale to tell, showed signs of being misinterpreted by that same foolish public. The Prince was the injured party; but the public booed him, and cheered the Princess.

He waited at Brighton for the decision which would surely show who was right in this matter, and who wrong.

And, when the strain became too great, sought solace with the unfailing Lady Hertford.

The news, when it came, was incredible.

The Princess of Wales had been acquitted of any charge

of having given birth to an illegitimate child.

True, a rider was added that her behaviour in several other respects was liable to 'very unfavourable interpretations', and her servants' reports must be credited 'until they shall receive some decisive contradiction'. Colourful reports they were; and although the taking of evidence had purportedly been done in the strictest privacy, details were not long in seeping out. The servants, suitably rewarded, talked as freely outside as they had done inside. It was reported that the Princess received her lovers gartered below the knee; that if Sir Sydney Smith or Captain Manby or some young naval officer from Greenwich were not available, she would entertain the servants themselves; that she floundered about on satin cushions after discarding her stays and loosening her clothes, interspersing her dalliance with ale and onions; and that she titillated her chosen guests with specially commissioned lewd drawings. There was talk of George Canning. There was so much talk of Sir Thomas Lawrence that a number of young matrons hastily cancelled portrait sittings that had been arranged. There was, indeed, talk of almost everyone.

Yet she was acquitted of the most serious charge, which could have cast doubt on the rightful succession to the English throne and caused complications in royal rights in Hanover; and the people cheered.

The only satisfaction the Prince might derive from the whole business was that the King found the Commission's comments disturbing enough to warrant his forbidding the Princess of Wales to be received at Court.

It was a satisfaction more than counterbalanced, though, by another of his father's prohibitions. Fox, weighted down with dropsy, had died after only a short spell in the Ministry of All the Talents. His day for high office had come too late. The Prince hurried to London for the service in Westminster Abbey, only to be told that the King forbade him to attend. Even with Fox dead there was to be no royal forgiveness.

The final injury was inflicted when the King decided that for his daughter-in-law there might, after all, be forgiveness. His decision was not entirely spontaneous. One of Caroline's staunchest allies throughout the Delicate Investigation, Spencer Perceval, had come into a new Tory government formed after Lord Grenville had bowed out; but as one of the terms of his appointment had insisted that a public reconciliation should be made between the King and the Princess.

'A snivelling Tory from Blackheath says who shall and shall not be received at Court!' exploded the Prince to his brother William. 'And Canning behind the two of them. The Cabinet's full of her drivelling weaklings. I know the constipated canary Perceval has written all those sly letters of hers, asking for my father's "gracious protection". And "great clemency" – can you imagine that onion-stuffed Brunswick cow thinking up such words for herself? An English cow might moo for gracious protection and clemency, but where would a German cow learn such things? And if he grants her wishes and receives her, then by God he'd better enlist the help of cowhands. For she'll foul his carpets. But one thing is still sure – she'll never set her hoofs on mine.'

In spite of his fury against his father for such slights and treacheries, the Prince knew it would be impolitic to retaliate by ignoring the summons to the royal birthday reception, much as he wished to do so.

Buckingham House was ablaze with light. The coaches of the guests were newly painted, the coachmen wore nosegays and streamers in their hats, and cheering crowds surged along the Mall. Arriving glumly and offering florid but equally glum birthday respects to his father, the Prince brightened up after circulating for a few minutes among old friends. He could never long remain uncommunicative in a party atmosphere. He kissed his mother, and she responded warmly: there was unspoken agreement between them on many a delicate subject, and especially so on the indelicate one which they had both so long hated. There were his sisters, too: delighted to see him and fuss over him, and growing up quite handsomely, he was pleased to observe.

Also present was the vivacious Lady Bessborough. He had known her for a quarter of a century, knew her children and grandchildren: how was it that he had never noticed before what a shapely creature she was, with such a proud carriage and such sparkling eyes? One day soon, perhaps, he would remedy his neglect. He had need of some diversion.

But for that, of course, Lady Hertford was more immediately accessible. He had been preparing his ground skilfully. Now he moved through the throng towards her, only to find her husband doing the same from another corner of the room.

Hastily the Prince slapped the Duke of York's breeches and nodded a plea for him to intercept Lord Hertford.

'Ah,' He reached Isabella. 'Your husband and my brother seem to have some mutual interests.'

'I believe the Duke felt Your Royal Highness's hand on his breeches.'

'For what reason, pray?' Her unflinching gaze mocked him, and he abandoned pretence. 'Perhaps I need some time with you.'

'I am honoured, as ever.'

'This evening there's too great a crush. Might I suggest that the gentleman who nudged the Duke of York would most deeply enjoy a visit from the Marchioness of Hertford tomorrow, in calmer surroundings? Carlton House tomorrow, say, starting with luncheon?' Surreptitiously he squeezed her hand. 'You are under pressure.'

'It is not unpleasant, your Royal Highness.'

This settled, the Prince returned to the company of his sisters for a while, noting at closer range that Amelia, his father's favourite, looked pale and drawn. She would have been better off in the quiet of her own room; but, like himself, though for more loving reasons, had felt she must attend the birthday festivities.

Suddenly an announcement resonated through the room.

'Her Royal Highness the Princess of Wales.'

George tried not to flinch. A deliberate affront, that she should be asked to the same function as himself! There was a respectful hush; some ladies curtsied; there was a murmur of greetings as the King and Queen received Caroline. To drown the obnoxious falsity of it all, the Prince said loudly to Princess Elizabeth:

'I swear I heard the mooing of a domestic animal. But I see no cowhand.'

'Be careful, George. She's coming across to us.'

'Then my bounden duty is to protect my sisters from this farmyard stray.'

In every quivering nerve he felt her approach; knew when she was close to his right elbow, and when heads were turning to watch; and dramatically turned his back to address his sister Amelia.

'Is it tethered? Eh? Am I safe? I hear no bell a-ding-a-ling-ing. It's long past milking time. Will no one fetch George Canning?'

There was no need for him to raise his voice. All other conversations in the room were a mumbled pretence. From a distance he heard his father trying to make out what was happening.

'Where is my little Charlotte?'

'She isn't here,' said the Queen. 'Caroline has come on her own.'

'Why?'

'It's all very confusing.'

'I am the one who's supposed to be confused.' The King's wailing protest rose more clamorously than his son's. 'Will no one tell me why this lunatic behaviour is sent to plague me? Eh? Well?'

'Do be calm, dearest.'

'I cannot hear a word,' shouted the King. 'What are you

all talking about? I cannot see, I cannot understand. Am I King of England, or am I not? Eh?'

Now everyone began to talk at once. When the King was discreetly led away, nobody gave any indication of noticing. More wine was poured. More laughter bubbled energetically up.

The Prince of Wales, his appetite for celebrations gone, found it more agreeable to make his excuses and depart early than to spend an uncomfortable evening avoiding his swaggering, cackling Princess of Wales. He retired to bed in Carlton House with the comfort of a bottle. A pity, he thought when the wine was finished, that he had not made his assignation with Lady Hertford for tonight. She would have soothed him.

In the morning his appetite was further soured. Isabella Hertford sent round by hand a note saying that she could not, on second thoughts, have luncheon with him. There was no explanation.

He responded with an urgent note, telling her that he was ill, that her missive had agitated him greatly; and instructed the messenger to impress on the Marchioness that the Prince was truly very pale and had had to take to his bed.

Lady Hertford appeared at Carlton House shortly after noon.

'Your Royal Highness.' She stood well back from the foot of the bed, her hands hidden within a muff, her eyes unfathomable behind a short lace veil.

'Isabella, thank God you've come.' The Prince subsided against his pillows. 'I am ill. I am on a diet of only French beans and barley water.'

'So sudden?' said that sensual, sceptical voice.

'Only you are to know. These afflictions come on me without warning. Mine is a nervous and delicate fibre. The disorders of my body owe much to the fever of my mind.'

'Your mind is perfectly clear.'

He patted the bed cover. 'Come.'

Slowly she advanced and lowered herself beside him.

She freed her hands and lifted her veil; but her eyes remained quizzical and amused.

The Prince complained: 'I do not understand your note. What are these second thoughts about our luncheon?'

'Mrs Fitzherbert is not present at the moment.'

The Prince feigned an inspection of the room. 'To the best of my knowledge she's in Brighton.'

'Then it is not proper I should lunch with you. It would be correct only if Mrs Fitzherbert were present. I have a reputation to protect.'

'Isabella, someone in your position has little need of such conventions.' He leaned forward so that his hand could creep across the bedclothes. 'Or is it that you want her here so that you may make sport – make her the slightest bit uncomfortable?'

'You have no grounds for such levity.'

'Do you not aspire to be her rival?'

There was a pause. But Lady Hertford was not moving away from his hand. 'That is your affair,' she said evenly.

'Isabella, I yearn for you.' It was true. Truer that he yearned for this magnificent woman more than he had ever yearned for a woman before. 'I am sick, I am positively ill because of you.'

He had her in his grip now. Running one hand along her cheek, he turned her face towards his. When he kissed her she did not move, but seemed to taste him and assess him according to some standard of her own. Her standards in everything were, he adoringly surmised, so high.

When he released her she said: 'Ill, your Royal Highness? You kiss with a very healthy tongue. Very prettily.'

But no, she would not stay for luncheon.

The Prince realized she was serious in her insistence on a chaperon. It was absurd. There would soon be a time, there had to be, when he would be with her and would possess her, and on such an occasion the presence of a chaperon would be too ludicrous an idea. But for public appearances together she was not yet going to allow herself to be compromised.

Then Maria must invite her more often. And must be here when he invited Lady Hertford. Maria, after all, was greatly in the Hertfords' debt.

When he returned to Brighton it was to find Minnie Seymour with her guardian waiting for him.

'I'm here to thank you, sir.'

'Whatever for, pray?'

She thought he was teasing, and was expecting her to play up to him. She drew herself up solemnly. It was not easy for her: in her muslin and frills and ringlets she was too light, too impish, too volatile to have learned solemnity. With a catch of gaiety in her manner she said:

'For my new gold charm. And the cakes you sent me. The almanacs. The ear-rings, and the essence box.'

He swept her up in his arms and hugged her. 'How I love you, my magical Minnie. Love you better than anyone in the world, you hear me?' He went on hugging her until she gasped and squealed and begged to be put down.

And it was true that he loved her, adored her. She had always been his special pet. For a while he had forgotten her, he had been preoccupied, there was so much on his mind; but he had sent her the presents, and now that he was with her again she enchanted him once again.

Maria Fitzherbert smiled and shook her head reprovingly.

'Now, angel.' The Prince set the little girl down. 'Run through that door and find a servant. Ask him to take you to my study, and to my desk. On my desk is a bowl of fresh peaches. Instruct the man to make you a bowl of peaches, cream and sugar. Then I want you to look at my snuff-boxes. From those of gold and enamel I want you to decide which you judge the most beautiful of all. The two most beautiful. Then bring them back here to me.'

When Minnie had scampered away on this fresh treasure hunt, the Prince set himself to change his clothes. For a few minutes Maria sat watching him with a curious tilt of her head. Then, breathing a cryptic little sigh, she came to him to adjust his white neckcloth, which threatened to spray outwards in a great rolling breaker.

He said: 'By the bye, Minnie's aunt asks after her.'

Her fingers hesitated for an instant. 'And how is the Lady Hertford?'

'Well. One dines with her.'

'One dines?'

'*En famille*, of course. With Lord Hertford. Always *en famille*. Such taste, the two of them. Such exquisite paintings.'

'Paintings. Yes, of course.'

'We must invite her in return. To talk about Minnie.' When Maria did not reply, he stooped before the glass to settle his powdered wig more securely, and said: 'You're thinking . . . ?'

'Nothing.'

He could not leave it at that. Some dangerous impulse drove him to continue the conversation, as one would venture out on a tightrope from sheer bravado rather than necessity.

'Maria, you know you're the one I love. But I don't expect you to be in attendance on me every hour of the day. I don't insist on imprisoning your affections.'

'Might I not wish to be so imprisoned?'

'When you think of it' – he tried to make it jovial and uncomplicated – '*I* am the one who's imprisoned. A prisoner of my so-called whore wife. It could drive me mad. But I must ask God not to let me go the way of the King, eh? He is madder.'

She was listening, but gave the impression of hearing something beyond what he was actually saying. The more he boomed on, the sadder became her smile.

It was a relief when Minnie came dancing back in with two snuff-boxes, one in each hand.

'They're so beautiful.'

The Prince took them from her, one in each of his own hands, and put his hands behind his back.

'Now. Which hand?'

Minnie dabbed at him, withdrew her hand, then risked a firm tap on his left elbow.

'Good.' He handed her the box, with its little porcelain inlay of roses and green foliage. 'And now this one.' He brought his other hand from behind his back. 'Take this to Maria.'

Minnie offered the box to her guardian, beaming delightedly up into her face so that Maria had to emulate her excitement and anticipation.

The lid of this one carried a fine, tiny portrait of the Prince of Wales. Mrs Fitzherbert looked at it; and smiled at Minnie, but could not raise her eyes to the prince himself.

He said: 'Well, now. I will arrange for you to be shown out.' He put a hand on Maria's shoulder, and nodded at the snuff-box. 'Rather fine, isn't it? Little minx, she chose one of my best. Well, there it is: a present for you, my dear. Worth a great deal of money.'

At the door he bellowed for a footman.

Maria Fitzherbert remained for a few moments where she was, her head lowered, as Minnie rubbed delightedly against her. The wits had cause for their jibe that, with the aid of Lady Hertford, Mrs Fitzherbert had won a child but lost a husband.

The harpsichord jangled as King George's gnarled fingers clawed over wrong chords and thumped down at shattering discords. He tried to sing to his own accompaniment, but for the words he babbled no music had even been composed.

'York will not have command of the Army in Spain. No, ha ha. Nor Cumberland. And as for Clarence – no, William, no command of the Mediterranean fleet. Kent's not for Gibraltar. All understood, eh, what-what? And I know about you, Frederick. Selling commissions, you and your doxy – crooked conniving criminal. My Frederick! But I *know*, I know it all.' His head fell forward against the marquetry panel, and he howled. Then, waiting for the echoes within the instrument to die away, he apologized most abjectly to it. 'I'm sorry. I know that hurt. Please speak to me. And speak for me, somebody. They'll come for me again, you know.'

Yes, they would soon be coming. He knew it, felt it. The Prince of Wales wanted to be Regent, and that awful boy always got his own way. No way of stopping him. He had tried hard, but there was no way of controlling that boy.

The King heaved himself up under the lid of the harpsichord. The strings cut into his palms. A ghostly shiver of strange harmonics sighed away into infinity. But they wouldn't find him in here. None of them would ever find him now.

He tried to pull the lid shut on top of himself as the door creaked open.

Queen Charlotte took a step into the room, let out one instinctive sob, then quickly closed the door behind her.

'George, it's all right, dearest.'

'They're coming for me.'

'No, George. Let me help you.'

'Everyone's coming for me.'

The Queen sidled up to the instrument and tried to get her arm under his chest and turn him over so that he could slide out and on to his feet again. She gasped.

'It's wet. The strings . . . and George, you're wet.'

'I couldn't wait,' he wailed. 'All those doses, the purgatives, everything they pour into me . . . Go away, leave me alone. I want nothing more. Nothing, ever. I do not wish to stay in this world.'

She struggled to free him – or capture him. She was not sure which, and neither was the King.

Wherever he sought support, it gave way beneath him.

When he tried to cling to sanity, it slid jeeringly away from him. His favourite son, the Duke of York, had been found by the House of Commons not guilty of conspiring with his mistress to sell commissions in the Army; but, with so many still accusing him of malpractice, had chosen to resign as Commander-in-Chief. There had been an attempt on the Duke of Cumberland's life in his rooms at St James's Palace, and the tongues of the town wagged through any number of discreditable explanations of the affair. The official story was that the valet, deranged, had tried to murder his master with a sabre but, failing, was chased off with a poker and then committed suicide. A more popular version had the Duke, for some mysterious but undoubtedly sinister motive, killing the valet himself. Unlike his brothers, the Duke had never had any permanent liaison – or, indeed, any known liaison at all – with one of the opposite sex. He invited few people to his suite in the palace; and there were dark tales of the kind of people he did then invite.

It was all too much for the King to grapple with. 'I do not hear this tale of blood aright. I see only fire and the faces of dying angels. And I see the people of this kingdom all walking in their sleep to the north, to ice on fire, and the armies of the East sit in wait in the trees . . .'

Then the consumption which had been wasting his favourite daughter Amelia away made its last fierce attack, and Amelia was dead. Reason fled the King; this time for the last time.

CHAPTER SEVEN

Lady Bessborough, rolling naked in the Prince's bed to display her ample if ageing breasts, said: 'You say you need someone to trust. But who can trust *you*?'

Sated, he abstractedly caressed the pleasures he had so recently enjoyed. 'I love you, Henrietta.'

'You make a fair pretence, that I'll grant.'

'I've loved you so long without showing it. I shall always love you.'

'And Isabella Hertford?'

'We share many artistic tastes. But I fear she likes only to be close to the throne.'

'The way things are going with His Majesty, she seems likely to be very close, very soon.'

The Prince kissed her ear. 'She's a tyrant.'

'But you have asked her to live with you publicly.'

The Prince jolted up in bed. 'Who says that?'

'It is common talk.'

'If I had ever had such a passing thought . . .'

'On the subject of passing thoughts, what of me?'

'You? Your body excites me more than any other.'

To his surprise, Lady Bessborough lurched out of bed, tugging a sheet around herself and stumbling over one end of it.

'I'm not a whore,' she blazed.

'But you have a harlot's skills. I adore it.'

'Then go and hire yourself one.'

'Henrietta.' His tone was injured. 'I beg you show kindness to me. I am greatly perplexed, I am not well, I have no one to turn to.'

'What of Mrs Fitzherbert?'

'Oh, Mrs Fitz . . .' He heard the treacherous dismissal in

his own head, and was horrified. But immediate satisfaction was, like the desire of every true artist, of more importance than any long-lasting placidity. 'That's past. We'll always be good friends, of course, but neither of us owes the other anything. I need someone who — '

'You make yourself ill lusting after Hertford. You regard me as a willing substitute. And you're the kind of man who fancies himself as Prince Regent? Pah!'

Really, women were so unreasonable. He said: 'I beg you to stay, Henrietta. What arrangements can I make for you? Canning – yes, I'll speak with Canning about you.'

'You'll do no such thing.'

'I can make a settlement to make things easier for you, if that's what you need.'

'Money? I am *not* your whore!'

And Lady Bessborough was not the only one to prove unreasonable. There seemed to be times in a man's life when everyone, and especially women, turned against him. This was one of them. He needed perfect calm in which to contemplate the renewed problems of his father's illness – a calm in which such frenzies would not attack him, too – yet just at this time all those who should be soothing him were turning on him.

Seeking distraction, he invited Lady Hertford to dinner; but, in answer to her wary question, had to hurry off a summons to Maria Fitzherbert to come up to town from her house in Brighton.

Her reply was incredible. She wrote, in that girlishly rounded hand he had once known so well but which in years of intimacy he had rarely seen, since there was little need for written communication, that she could no longer demean herself by playing the 'scandal blanket' for him.

> I have been put in a position that is undignified and unacceptable to me. The great incivilities I have received just because I obeyed your orders have been too visible to everyone present, and too poignantly felt by me to

admit of my putting myself in a situation of being treated with such indignity, for whatever may be thought of me by some individuals, it is well known your Royal Highness four and twenty years ago placed me in a situation so nearly connected with your own that I have a claim on you for protection. But now the comfort and happiness of both our lives are destroyed so that neither our health nor our spirits can stand any more. No other can surpass the affection I have for you, but I can never submit to appear in your house in any place or situation but in that where you first placed me many years ago.

I remain, with all my good wishes,
very sincerely,
Maria.

Tears coursed freely down the Prince's cheeks, and plopped from the wide expanse of his chin on to the page below, blurring the ink.

CHAPTER EIGHT

The Prince sat with his brothers in his study at Carlton House. Momentous decisions were in the air. He was determined that they should be the right ones: he was not going to be slighted again, nor have unacceptable limitations imposed on him. If Perceval and his administration wanted a Regent, they should have one. But they should not be presented with a puppet.

He said: 'I'm sure you agree that restrictions cannot be arbitrarily imposed on my powers.'

'It's out of the question,' said the Duke of Cumberland. 'That you be prohibited the opportunity to create peers.'

'The draft suggestions do allow for the creation of some peers,' the Duke of York pointed out: 'military and naval commanders.'

'Who probably won't live long enough to celebrate the honour,' said the Duke of Clarence.

'It will make not just me but all of us look foolish if such appointments are conditional upon the King's pleasure for their continuance.' The Prince looked round the faces of his brothers and found no sign of dissent.

The Duke of Cumberland leaned forward so that light intensified the ugly weals where his valet's sabre had sliced down his face. His left cheek puckered hideously inwards as if he were sucking dubiously at some unpalatable sweetmeat. 'And who is to manage father's household, since he's no longer capable of doing so himself? Provisions have been made for you to take it over, George?'

'No,' said the Prince of Wales. 'Not I.'

'Then who?'

'Mother. The Queen.'

'But that's ridiculous.'

'There are too many ridiculous aspects to this whole business,' agreed the Prince.

While he had the Royal Dukes under his roof and, on this subject if on no other, in broad general agreement with him, the Prince had a letter drawn up and signed by all of them. It protested to Spencer Perceval, the Prime Minister, against any limitation of the Prince's power in the event of a Regency, as being in defiance of the principles on which the House of Hanover succeeded to the throne of England. Perceval doggedly announced that he intended to proceed nevertheless; but the limitations would last for only a year. The Tories hoped that during that year the King would once more recover. The Whigs publicly wished the King such a speedy recovery; but covertly hoped otherwise.

The Regency Bill was passed by a narrow majority. Whig protests against the limitations did not, however, strike the Prince of Wales as having been framed nearly strongly enough.

If only Fox had been alive at this hour!

Grey and Grenville were cold fish, unreliable, and not good company. There was only one of his old drinking companions left.

He sent for Sheridan, and opened a bottle; and then opened another.

'I will not be dictated to by the freaks and caprices of anyone.' Here in the sumptuous colours and warmth of his study, he could be regal and forceful, damning Parliament and all its grubby place-seekers. 'I shall bide my time, and then tell the country what is good for it. In the meantime, I have something in mind for you, old friend.'

'The Treasury?' asked Sheridan doubtfully. 'Or the Foreign Secretaryship? You know I've always fancied myself as — '

'How about Secretaryship of Ireland, eh?'

Sheridan stared over his glass. 'Is that an order, a request, or a joke?'

'A little present for you. Or it was to have been. But your supposed friend Grey tells me that your appointment would be tantamount to sending a man with a lighted torch into a magazine of gunpowder.'

'And Grey is supposed to be of our own party! When *he* comes to office — '

'*If* he comes to office.' The Prince drank deeply, to give himself courage to tell Sheridan what had to be told. 'Things may not be to our liking yet awhile. If Grey and Grenville and the rest – no, not you, old friend, you did nobly – if the rest of them had spoken out firmly enough, they might still have carried the day. As it is, I am tied hand and feet for twelve months. Two of my brothers think the Tories should stay. So do my sisters. In his few lucid moments my father might suffer irreparable harm if he heard that we had tried too much, too soon. The Hertfords favour the Tories.'

'The Hertfords,' growled Sheridan, 'have never favoured anyone other than the Tories.'

The Prince shrugged. He refilled his glass and then found that he had no wish for more wine. The years had slipped away faster than he cared to recall, carrying with them his appetite for drunkenness and late hours of debauchery and argument. Without Fox, argument had lost its savour. The civilized company of the patrician Hertfords, with their talk of painting and sculpture and music, was more to his taste nowadays. Regretfully he set the glass down.

And there had not been a lady in his bed for many a night now. Thoughts of the Regency had occupied his pillow, and would be with him again tonight.

'I'll reinstate Frederick as Commander-in-Chief,' he mused.

'And something for yourself?' said Sheridan acutely.

'Many a lonely night I've debated that. You know, sensible women – handsome, bulksome, well-back-sided women – they like a man to be a big man, in a big and splendid uniform. I shall promote myself Field-Marshal.'

F

'Splendid.' Sheridan raised his glass. He showed no reluctance to continue drinking, and surveyed his old friend with placidly bleary eyes. 'That will be your masterpiece.'

The swearing-in of the Regent had to be planned with some tact. It would have been inappropriate to stage a sumptuous ceremony in Westminster Abbey, with the implication that the King was as good as dead, long live the new King. Pomp and rejoicing accorded ill with George III's darkening miseries. It was suggested that the formalities should be contained within Carlton House, to which the Prince of Wales readily assented. But within those familiar halls and salons he set himself to provide as lavish a background as was consonant with the regrettable circumstances of his elevation. The band of the Grenadier Guards was engaged to play marches in the garden, interspersed at intervals with a respectful rendering of 'God Save the King'. And the Princess Charlotte was also relegated to the garden, with two grooms in attendance. At fifteen she was growing into an attractive but pert and peppery girl, uncomfortably like her mother in freedom of speech and ready impertinence, in spite of the Prince's efforts to keep contact between them to a minimum. He did not fancy her attendance at the actual ceremony indoors: there was no telling what she might come out with, or what the assembled dignitaries might make of her.

She challenged him: 'What about Mama?'

'What about her?'

'Will she be playing some part in this swearing?' The girl's grin, sly and provocative, twisted her lips down at one end just as Caroline's lips had all too often twisted. 'She's good at swearing.'

'You are not to speak of your mother like that. And it's not a swearing, but a swearing-in. And she will not play any part in it.'

'You hate her, don't you?' said Charlotte.

'No. That is — '

'She hates you.'

'I hope,' he said feebly, 'she doesn't really mean it.'

She stared candidly at him. Then her smile grew a trifle wistful. 'Do you hate me, Papa – hate me because of her?'

'No,' he cried.

She looked neither pleased nor querulous. But he was glad to escape that disconcerting gaze and return to matters with which he felt more at home – pomp, grandeur, ceremonial, colour, the urge to do always the best in every possible way. It was all he had ever wanted: the best.

On 5th February 1811 the grand salon was dominated by a broad, long table covered in red velvet. An army of silver inkstands was arrayed down it, one for each chair. The Yeomen of the Guard and the Prince's servants in full livery were standing to attention along the walls. Banks of flowers filled the air with an early spring fragrance.

In the garden there was a sharp command, and the band stopped playing in the middle of a bar. Then there was a protracted drum roll.

The doors of the salon were thrown open, and the Prince advanced majestically, bearing the weight of his new Field-Marshal's uniform and the glittering decorations which had, some of them, been presented by foreign allies, but most of them of his own devising. When he had reached the head of the table there was a fanfare of trumpets, and his brothers stood behind their chairs, waiting for the Bishops and Privy Councillors to take their allotted places.

The band began to play another rousing march.

At a window appeared, briefly, the Princess Charlotte. In her green riding habit and a straw hat laced under her stubborn chin, she was pushing herself up from the saddle, mouthing something. It was impossible to tell whether she was wishing her father well or ill. Then she was coaxed away by her attendants.

There came a kissing of hands, a long procession, and a few apprehensive glances from Canning and Perceval at the massive bust of Charles James Fox on a plinth behind the Prince's chair.

Whispers of movement died away. The Prince rose to his feet.

'I, George Augustus Frederick, Prince of Wales, Earl of Chester, Duke of Cornwall, Duke of Rothesay, Earl of Carrick and Baron of Renfrew, will truly and faithfully execute the office of Regent of the United Kingdom of Great Britain and Ireland, to consult and maintain the safety, honour and dignity of His Majesty the King and the welfare of his people.'

How long would it be before he could enter into his full birthright as true, complete and inarguable King?

PART FOUR

REGENT AND KING

CHAPTER ONE

The Whigs had been waiting so long for power. Now at last, as the first year of the limited Regency drew to a close and it was plain that King George III would never recover his faculties, they waited for the Regent to be freed of restrictions and grant them their reward.

But the radical fires which had once burned in the Prince were dimmed. If Charles James Fox had been alive to fan the embers to flame again, he might have tipped out the Tories and formed a new administration. But Fox was dead; and Lady Hertford was very much alive. The Prince Regent decided to retain Perceval as Tory Prime Minister, but asked if some representatives of his old coterie would accept office in a patriotic coalition. The Whig leaders, Grey and Grenville, haughtily refused. The war against Napoleon was dragging on, and Wellington in the Peninsula was achieving victories only at an enormous cost in money and equipment. People at home were near starvation. The Whigs demanded reform at home and a sensible settlement abroad. Perceval and Lord Liverpool stuck to their guns. The Prince Regent, with Lady Hertford to strengthen his resolve, decided to stand by them.

The bile of the cartoonists, once so sourly lavished on Mrs Fitzherbert, was now spat in Lady Hertford's direction; and there was a series of attacks on the Prince's renewed extravagance now that his powers were so much increased and his father no longer capable of checking them. But he had weathered such storms of abuse before, and could weather them again. Political bickering, once stimulating, was now tedious. The Prince Regent turned his attention once more to the arts, always more rewarding than Parliamentary and social problems. He closeted himself with the admirable Mr Nash, who had stepped into the shoes of the late Henry Holland as his favourite architect, and pored over plans for adding new splendours to London. Their new concepts must rival anything so far achieved in Paris or Vienna. They talked of parks and a canal; of a royal mile of graceful terraces culminating in a colonnade at Carlton House; and of villas, lakes and gateways. There would be a Regent's Park and a Regent Street.

And when London had been nobly transformed, then it would be time to reconsider those long-delayed plans for expanding his pavilion at Brighton. France's 'Sun King' had once set a standard of elegance admired by the world. Britain should have her 'Sun Prince', then. And perhaps with new architecture, exotic new colours and panels and traceries and hangings, it would be possible to banish some of the uncomfortable ghosts who persisted in haunting certain rooms in the pavilion.

When the gossips tired of Lady Hertford and speculated that surely the Prince Regent must also by now be tiring of her, they looked around to see where else his interests might fall. For once the woman making the most serious demands on his attention was not a grandmother. She was much younger than he: hardly surprising, since she was his daughter.

At sixteen the Princess Charlotte looked twenty. She had wild tow-coloured hair, a fine impertinent toss of the head, the petulant Hanoverian mouth, a boyish energy but a womanish glow; and a suspicion of a stammer. This impediment was most marked when she was in her father's company. At other times it was hardly noticeable.

The Queen had some observations to make on this score.

'The girl talks too much, George. And worse, she intersperses quite polite conversation with *words*.'

'I think everyone brings words into conversation,' said her son mildly, 'either side of the silences.'

'This is a serious matter. She uses words describing

various parts of the body. The masculine body. And . . . and functions, as well.'

'What functions?'

'Bodily functions,' said the Queen, denunciatory. 'They're quite irregular.'

'Charlotte's functions – irregular? She has a perfectly good physician. Or is the cook at fault?'

'I mean that the words are irregular.'

'As long as her functions are in order I can't see the words matter.'

The Queen drew another breath and went off on another task. 'She also shows her drawers.'

'To whom?'

'To whomsoever chooses to look at them.'

'Mother.' The Prince Regent heaved himself to his feet, wriggling his great bulk to ease the constriction of his corset. 'I didn't come down to Windsor simply to hear that my daughter speaks words and exhibits her drawers. The matter of the moment is that of a husband.'

'You think it's time to marry her off?'

'Don't you?'

'High time,' said the Queen.

There had already been talk in the family about a number of undesirable suitors with whom Charlotte, bored by life in her strictly supervised royal residences, had fallen impetuously in love. Least desirable had been one Captain Hesse of the Hussars. He was a bastard son of the Duke of York, which in itself made any relationship with the Princess undesirable. He was also known to visit the Princess of Wales, and it came to the Prince's ears that this detestable woman had not hesitated to test the fellow's prowess in bed before deciding whether to condone his courtship of her daughter. The final straw was the revelation that Hesse was a regular courier between mother and daughter: not only did he boldly visit Caroline in the Kensington Palace rooms misguidedly set aside for her by the King during the period of their wary reconciliation, but carried long and scurrilous letters from her to Charlotte when the girl was staying at Windsor – a correspondence strictly forbidden by her father.

Hesse must be sent packing. But Charlotte's youthful impatience was such that a substitute must be found; and found soon.

CHAPTER TWO

The Prime Minister had been murdered in the lobby of the House.

When the news reached the Prince Regent, it was accompanied by the disquieting information that the assassin firing the fatal shot had done so in protest against the war and what it had done to him. A merchant by the name of Bellingham, he complained of having been bankrupted, and there was the strong implication that he had acted on behalf of thousands of other sufferers throughout the land.

The Prince was outraged; and alarmed. How many fanatics were roaming the streets, ready to take desperate measures? He felt a pulse begin to beat in his forehead, and tried to calm himself.

To whom could he now entrust his Government? Canning hated Castlereagh, and the antipathy was said to be mutual. In any case the Prince had his own reasons for viewing Canning with mistrust. But his old instinct to turn to a reliable Whig had been blunted long ago. Only a year or so, really, but it seemed an eternity. It would not be to Grey or any of his associates that he would turn for advice.

It would have to be Lady Hertford.

Summoned to Carlton House, she found the Prince in an unusual and ungainly position. In an effort to numb the mental and physical distress brought on by this deplorable situation, he had imbibed rather more brandy that he was accustomed to nowadays and, swaying across his study, had come down heavily and twisted an ankle. Neither the brandy nor the fall had done his gout any good; which was why he now lay propped up in bed with his right leg encased in bandages and held out at an awkward angle by a contraption of wires and pulleys.

Lady Hertford contemplated the bizarre scene with motherly solicitude, then settled herself at the Prince's bedside and offered him a ripe peach.

'Poor Perceval,' she said without preamble.

'Poor Perceval be damned. He's the only one of us who doesn't have to worry himself to death any more.'

'So you're worried?'

'Of course I'm worried. Violence all around us. And a Parliament without a Prime Minister. What do we do to replace Perceval?'

It was clear that she had come primed with the right answers. Without hesitation she said: 'Liverpool. It has to be.'

'But the man's a weakling. Not an idea in his head. Hopeless.'

'Lord Liverpool will do better than you think. Much better. You need him.'

'Isabella, it's you I need. I've absorbed laudanum, laudanum, and laudanum. When what would cure me swiftest would be you: your body, your soul, your everything.'

'Laudanum and maraschino and peaches.' Lady Hertford surveyed the row of decanters on the bedside table. 'And brandy and gin and sherry. A heady mixture. And now me too.'

'You above all, Isabella. To give me the strength to deal with all these disorders. Murderers here, slanderers there. Danger abroad and at home. Oh, the Government has been prosecuting the war reasonably well. But there are troublemakers in our midst. This Bellingham madman. And those Irish who are coming to the boil again. One can be sure of one thing about the English monarchy: for ever, so long as there's an English throne for some poor wretch to put his or her buttocks on, all kings and queens of England will wish, desperately, that the Irish would go away and stay away. And d'you know what I know, that'll take future generations a long time to learn?'

'I have no idea.'

'The Irish never *will* go away. All these letters' – he ruffled a disordered heap of paper on the bed – 'must be from Irishmen, or Bellinghams, or some singularly stupid folk in . . . oh, I don't know – Yorkshire, Suffolk, heaven knows where. Listen.' He began to recite in a pained voice. ' "Give us bread or you will be dead; Quit the country or you will lose your head." What base ingratitude is that? Signed "An Enemy of the Damned Royal Family," too. That I should have such enemies, after all I've tried to do – trying to beautify this land of ours and leave it so much finer than I found it! And look, here's someone who ought to know better. In The Examiner they refer to me as the Prince of Whales – with an "h", dammit – and write, "Not a fatter fish than he . . . Flounders round the polar sea." What do I do?'

Lady Hertford pondered. Then she said tranquilly: 'You appoint Lord Liverpool. And you arrange a royal marriage. The British love a royal marriage: it takes their minds off more troublesome things.'

'Splendid.' The Prince reached out rapturously for her, then winced as the wires tightened. 'I wouldn't object to one for myself, if I could get rid of that stinking wife of mine. Then, Isabella, you and I could have such a magnificent ceremony.'

'You appear to forget that I, too, am tied. I have a husband.'

'No way of getting rid of him?'

'Certainly not.'

The Prince had finished his peach and was wiping his fingers fastidiously on a napkin. 'Then it will have to be Charlotte. My mother and I have had it in mind for some little while. We must urge Charlotte towards the altar.'

'You have someone in mind to stand beside her?'

'Mm. It'll have to be someone helpful politically. Someone like young William of Orange.'

'Who looks,' said Lady Hertford authoritatively, 'like a drunken little frog.'

'At least he'll jump about.'

'He spent two years at Oxford,' she recalled. 'I'm told he was infected less by learned habits than by quite excessive jollity. A great deal of prancing up and down and crying "Oh-ho-ho" and such-like.' She eyed the Prince thoughtfully. 'What will Charlotte make of such a husband?'

'She'll make what she chooses. At the moment she's locked up with a selection of old hags who have orders to keep her in sight and out of mischief every hour of the day and night. I've been strict with her and with them. For her own good, you understand. Now she'll be only too glad to escape, even if it's only into the arms of a frog, or a toad, or a newt or any other species you care to provide.'

'And if you find she doesn't love him?'

'Oh, love – love is blind,' said the Prince inconsequentially. 'Save with me, Isabella. For I can see, and I love you. Unhinge this rack, will you? And kiss me.'

Lady Hertford carefully selected a plum from the bowl, placed it in his mouth, and then held her palm out so that he might spit the stone into it.

'When you go,' he threatened, his mouth full, 'I shall be ill again.'

But when she had in fact departed he lay back, easing himself into a less uncomfortable position, and thought what a sound idea it would be to arrange a marriage. There was little doubt about the bridegroom: the Prince of Orange was the man. Memories of the House of Orange would appeal to the majority of good Protestant Englishmen, if not to the eternally troublesome Irish. The political liaison would be most useful during the closing stages of the war and after.

Woe betide the girl if she raised any objections.

CHAPTER THREE

More letters exposing royal dissensions appeared in the press. This time, however, it was not the Prince of Wales sending them to further his cause against King George III: this time they were letters released to further the causes of the Princess of Wales and her daughter Charlotte. They showed the public that the Prince was cruelly keeping mother and daughter apart, did not propose to allow the mother to attend Charlotte's official coming-out when that was finally sanctioned, and intercepted even the most everyday communication between them. The two women were not allowed to meet for months on end, and then only under the most humiliating supervision. To these revelations the public reacted by booing the Queen and the Prince Regent whenever they passed, and cheering the two Princesses.

The Prince was furious at this calculated leakage of information, and intensified the watch on his daughter. Changes were made among her attendants, and as her seventeenth birthday approached Charlotte was alarmed by the news that she was likely to have a new and stricter governess. At that age, she insisted, she was entitled to a complement of ladies-in-waiting and a household of her own rather than a governess. Her father seemed to have forgotten his own impatience to be set up in an establishment of his own, all those years ago, and rejected all such possibilities . . . until she should marry. Then, and only then, would he condescend to free her from her bevy of female gaolers and let her create her own household.

In addition to the watching women, Charlotte received three or four visits a week from a bishop whose task was to elevate her mind. All attempts to speak to him on a human level, confiding in him as a friend and relying on his helpful advice, were in vain. The bishop talked resoundingly of the sanctity of marriage, her duties to the Church of England, and her duties to her country. No word of love, or even of liking.

His solemn lectures, together with her own observation of what marriage had meant to her mother and father, hardly endeared the notion of wedlock to Charlotte. But it was increasingly borne in on her that the nearest thing to independence she could hope for was in marriage.

When she gave way, and her betrothal to the Prince of Orange was announced, her mother was neither consulted nor invited to any of the planned festivities.

Disobeying all orders, Charlotte went to see her.

The reunion could have been a happier one. Caroline, besotted with her latest captive, a swarthy Italian musician whose accomplishments at the pianoforte were all too obviously secondary to his other talents, persisted in whiling away the evening in passionate solos and duets. Charlotte sat in a corner watching; and listening; and miserably wondering if, after all, there might not be some justification in her father's highhandedness. If only *he* had talked to her more, listened to her, relaxed with her, she would not have come running here.

A shrieking cadenza from her mother led to a dramatic glissando on the keyboard, and Sapio was applauding vigorously – applauding himself, one felt, as much as his companion.

'Bravo! Mosta exquisite. I am most totally ravished.'

'You're a flatterer, angel.'

Sapio leaned across the keyboard to seize Caroline's hand and kiss it extravagantly. 'I am mucha too modest, your Royal Highness. I only hear di truth, see di truth, speaka di truth.'

'You do all sorta of di mosta incredibler things,' Caroline mimicked him. Then she caught a glimpse of her daughter's withdrawn, unhappy expression, and was suddenly remorseful. 'That's enough, then. Do the most fantastic thing of all. Vanish – presto!'

When Sapio had made his departure in a series of sweeping bows and yearning waves of his arm, Princess Charlotte said coldly: 'He's an ourang-outang.'

'Hairy,' her mother conceded, 'but a brilliant musician.' She turned her attention full upon Charlotte, hurrying to her side and beginning to stroke her hair. 'You will see, my dear. The small men, they are the ones, they are the best. You are to have your William of Orange, yes? Little men like that are the most lascivious. Take him. Peel him.'

Charlotte jerked her head away from the fidgety caresses. 'Because you want Charles Hesse to yourself, Mama?'

'I want no man in particular,' said Caroline airily. 'Not your father, not —'

'You are Charles Hesse's lover?'

'Oh, my darling girl.' Caroline tried to touch her again, but again Charlotte edged aside. 'You're so young. No, I am nobody's lover. I give no man my love. I *eat* them.'

'I . . . I hope . . .' A hint of Charlotte's stammer was returning. 'I think you should go away. Soon.'

'Away?'

'Leave England.'

Caroline stood very still, then snorted a laugh. 'I think of it more than once. And why not? There is nothing here for me. Nothing but the pleasure of making a fool of your father and watching him make a fool of himself. And I can as well do that abroad. I will. Yes.'

'You'll f-find it more . . . restful.'

'But I do not wish to be restful. Oh, no. I will behave as the harlot of the world through all Europe, to discredit that buffoon.'

'Mother . . .'

'Nobody wants me here, and I want nothing here. You all wish me out of the way. You, too. I am an embarrassment, to you as well.'

'You are my mother,' said the Princess wretchedly.

'Do you love me because of that? Do you? It was snarled out.

'I wish I could. But I . . . I do not.'

Caroline tried to shrug it off. 'That is your father's fault, angel. Blame your father, not me, and then we speak no more of it. You are my daughter, so of course you love me.'

Charlotte stared at the piano as if she could still see the dark, lecherous little Italian at the keyboard; and, beyond him, a slavering host of others.

'I do not. And never will again.'

'You don't know what you're saying.'

'Oh, I do. I may not be sure of love. But hate is always clear and certain. One is sure one hates. It is such a definite emotion.'

'*Mein Gott,*' whispered her mother. 'You talk like an old woman.'

'And you look like one.'

'And you've grown into a bitch.'

'Perhaps I am that, too. I take after my mother.'

Before Caroline could say any more, Charlotte turned and ran from the room. It had been a mistake to come here, a mistake to hope for anything here. She would not come again.

It might have strengthened her, or terrified her, to have seen her mother's first act when she had left. From a drawer Caroline took out a little wax effigy with a grotesque little wig on it, and a caricature of the Regent's face cut from a print and stuck in place. She laid out a number of pins and began methodically, with the precision of long practice, sticking them into this representation of her husband.

Caroline, Princess of Wales, made up her mind. It was true that she had known few pleasures in this alien country, and that regrettably the most powerful one among them had been that of outraging the husband who had so outraged her. Other distractions had done no more than make life tolerable. The royal family had virtually disowned her. Her only protector, the King, was mad; the Queen had always despised her and now refused to receive her; she had rarely been allowed to see her own daughter unimpeded, and when they met they had usually quarrelled – this time, it was obvious, for the last time. She would not be allowed to attend the girl's wedding, would not meet visiting relatives from the Continent, and would be accorded none of the honour due to her. In Parliament she had supporters such as Brougham and Whitbread, but she suspected they were on her side only because they were opposed to the Prince. If she appeared at the opera, the audience cheered her; but as a sign of disrespect to the Prince rather than out of any instinctive love for herself. There was no love here, nothing she could rely on, no lasting loyalty.

Napoleon Bonaparte had been defeated. Europe was open once more to the traveller. She could go where she willed.

So she would leave.

Princess Caroline left England on an August day in 1814, taking with her a number of ladies-in-waiting, her chamberlain and equerry, and her beloved Willikin, now growing up into pampered adolescence. Also included in her entourage was young Captain Hesse. Gauche, gawky, immature Charlotte might think what she chose. Let the girl occupy herself with her Prince William of Orange.

CHAPTER FOUR

Charlotte did not wish to occupy herself with her Prince William of Orange. She looked at him through the glittering lights and swirling gowns, the coronets and jewels and decorations, the sumptuousness of the great Windsor Castle ballroom; and realized with sinking heart that every hour, every minute she liked less and less what she saw. The music was seductive: she would not be seduced. Couples spun and laughed and chattered through a waltz, though a few German and Austrian visitors were looking slightly puzzled: the English version was much more sedate than the lively tempo of the waltz to which they were accustomed in their own countries. But the Prince Regent was beaming at the orchestra and beating time, and beaming repeated encouragement at the slightly stooped young man beside him.

Prince William was, as everyone could see, drunk. He became easily and frequently drunk. He had already disgraced himself at Ascot and was obviously capable of doing so again in whatever setting his host provided.

Not, thought the Princess, that he was any more appealing when sober.

She must learn to like him. He was all she had to cling to. Of the other young men she had met, none had been treated with more than a curt dismissive wave from her father. Young Frog, as everyone at Court referred to Prince William, offered her escape from prison.

But into what other kind of captivity?

To her horror she saw that her father was steering William along one side of the ballroom towards her. She could not bear to watch that vacuous face approaching. But as she steeled herself to turn away, the view was momentarily blotted out by the voluminous puff sleeves and spreading hair of young Madame de Tatischeff, bowing and dropping a gentle curtsy to the Prince Regent.

'Chère madame.' The Prince graciously halted. *'Madame de Tatischeff, j'ai l'honneur de vous présenter — '*

'I say,' William burst out with that painfully acquired, and painful, accent which could surely not be endured year in, year out, through a whole lifetime, 'I'm William. William of Orange, ho-ho. And I see you're a ripe apple, what, ho-ho?'

The young woman extended a reluctant hand, which William seized and pumped heartily.

'Our young friend is a scholar, who has favoured our own Oxford,' said the Prince Regent. 'And a soldier of some distinction.'

'Very much a soldier.' William drew himself up and tried to click his heels, but narrowly avoided tripping himself up.

Madame de Tatischeff averted her head from the fumes of drink which he exuded. 'One always thought soldiers lacked the scholar's imagination and sensitivity.'

'Oh, jolly good, what? Quite a thought, ho-ho. May I have the infinite honour, madame, of accompanying you in a bit of the old one-foot-in-front-of-the-other . . . one, two, three, four, eh, ho-ho?'

'The waltz, sir, goes one-two-three.'

'Jolly good.'

Charlotte thankfully watched them stumble away. She hoped they would contrive to keep their feet until the music ended.

But the moment when she and Prince William danced together could not be forever postponed. When at last he came lurching towards her, the assembled company drew back into a respectful circle. There was a great expanse of floor across which the Princess and her partner must formally tread. And William was opening his arms as he approached, balancing himself with owlish concentration and grinning in what he must suppose to be an amorous invitation.

It was impossible. The whole thing was impossible. Charlotte turned her head away and walked briskly past him, almost brushing his shoulder but offering no excuse. An audible gasp followed her across the room.

Her father was standing beside Lady Hertford. He had summoned up a fond paternal smile to suit the occasion, but at the sight of his daughter cutting her betrothed dead it froze. He was speechless as she planted herself in front of him with legs straddled and her hands on her hips.

She said: 'You may tell the Young Frog to return to its lily-pad. I'll have no more to do with him.'

'But, my dear girl — '

'I suspected this was going to happen,' murmured Lady Hertford.

Before anyone could start making tactful remarks or try covering up the incident, try persuading her to turn back and make a joke of it with Prince William – which in his present sottish state he would probably accept – Charlotte strode out of the ballroom and left them to their buzz of gossip and malice and whatever hasty music might be summoned up to drown the echoes.

Three days later she received the summons she had been expecting.

Her father was striding up and down his study at Carlton House in a towering rage. He was colossal, and weighty and imposing, and ought in sheer bulk to have been terrifying. But the delay, in which Charlotte had been supposed to suffer remorse and apprehension and a sense of utter disgrace, had in fact given her time to compose herself. She stood well back, beside the window, to give him room for his pacing. And all at once, looking at him, she was strangely possessed by a feeling quite different from any she would have expected. She was not sorry for what she had done, but sorry for the position in which she had placed him. Sorry for him; and, without warning, absurdly fond of him.

'You've inherited the madness of your mother's blood,' he was storming. 'How could you have dared to insult the Prince of Orange so?'

'Much of his own behaviour was insulting,' said Charlotte calmly. 'He had so many undesirable aspects.'

'He's a young man, he has his faults, who hasn't? You've plenty of your own, my girl. But he is the Prince of Orange, and you have put him to shame before everyone.'

'His own conduct — '

'You, and you alone,' he roared, 'are responsible for him leaving England in a state of utter shame. Dear God Almighty, look at me. What I have to endure! Hissed at by the mobs, accused now of finding you a husband you've laughed at. How can I tell them it was for your own happiness? You've had a fine residence prepared in the Hague. Now it stands empty. You and your husband would have been royally housed in this country, too. But you have offended against England, and you've offended against Holland.'

'If all your bishop's precepts are right, then at least I have not offended against God.'

'Kindly leave God out of this.'

'I believe I have been true to myself and that only God may dictate love to that self.'

The Prince ceased his pacing and stared with mounting suspicion. 'What am I to understand by that? That all this time you've been cherishing other wayward ideas of your own?'

'It is early to say, father.'

'Say it, nevertheless, so I may know which way your insane fancies are likely to drive you.'

'I have several times met Leopold, as you know.'

'Leopold? Which one, dammit?'

'Leopold of Saxe-Coburg.'

'Good God, that one? Not a penny to his name. Poor as a church mouse.'

'Father, may I see him? And seriously consider the matter?'

'I will not have you throwing yourself away on a penniless schemer.'

'The Duke of York speaks highly of him. I know that Lord Castlereagh approves of him. And my dear friend Mercer Elphinstone, whom you yourself allowed to be appointed to my service – she thinks the world of him. It might be that I could love him.'

'What do you know of love?'

She heard herself saying, without premeditation and without doubt and without the slightest stammer: 'I know that I love you, father.'

His flushed countenance changed colour as if he had been winded in that vast, pendulous belly. He struggled for words. His lips quivered, and when at last he spoke he was choking with tears.

'You love me?'

She walked slowly towards him.

'But I adore you,' he cried. 'It may be hard for you to see. It . . . I . . . things have always gone wrong, haven't they? But whenever I see you, I want only for your happiness. Your complete happiness and contentment. You're all I have in this world – all that has lasted and will last.'

She took him in her arms and kissed him.

'Father, you've been so unhappy. Think of the joy there might be if I marry the man I love, a man I can love and respect, and we all share that love.'

'Are you sure of this Leopold?'

'I want your permission to see him, and for him to call upon you. Then in good time we shall learn what is to be.'

'Well.' The Prince turned his head away and wiped his eyes. He tried to reassert his authority. 'Very well. But I shall need time to think it over. I always take time, you know. Carefully. With due deliberation.'

'Yes, father.'

He consulted the carpet across which he had recently been wearing a track. 'Hm. Very well, I have thought it over. And I agree.'

She threw herself at him again, with such force that even his great body was almost carried backwards.

'Careful, angel,' he protested. 'I'm not one of your favourite horses, to be leapt upon like that.'

'Only a whale,' she laughed.

And this time for him it was a wonderful joke, not an insult. 'Quite a pretty whale, wouldn't you say?'

'The most beautiful in all the world.'

CHAPTER FIVE

Prince Leopold looked affectionately yet warily at the shy, awkward, slightly over-eager girl at his side; and even more warily at the box which she had laid out for his inspection on a table in the Carlton House conservatory. It was an elegant piece of carpentry and most elegantly adorned with the royal coat of arms. He was still as unsure of Princess Charlotte as she was unsure of herself. He smiled; she smiled diffidently back; and he wondered if she were proposing to play some gauche practical joke on him, releasing some jack-in-the-box in the hope of making him laugh and then bursting into girlish tears if he failed to respond.

She was so vulnerable. He wanted to take her wrist and coax her away and tell her not to risk absurdities: she had no need for such demonstrations.

Charlotte reached over the box to open the lid. 'I want you to like my best friends. It's so important that you should.'

He could not imagine what this had to do with the box. 'You still haven't told me their names.'

'Nod,' she said, 'and Wink.'

There were still so many secrets in her, and about her, to be disentangled. 'Are they very special friends?'

'Very.' She dipped her arm deep into the box. 'It's a bit strange, I suppose.' She stopped, quite still. 'I mean, you won't laugh at me – you won't, will you?'

'Of course not.'

'All right. But before I introduce you I must explain. It's serious. You do realize it's serious?'

'I do,' he said gently.

'It's serious,' she said, 'because this man and this woman

live in peace with each other. They move slowly. Hesitantly. They're very gentle. They are . . .' Her lips moved, then trembled. She was on the verge of stammering again, and he was afraid that if he tried to pick up a phrase to help her out he would only make it worse. 'Please don't laugh, Leopold. They're really everything I would like. For a father and m-mother, or . . . well . . . for myself. Gentle,' she said again. 'So gentle.'

'They're married?'

'Many years ago. I believe they were married one hundred years ago. They're most blissfully happy.' She was studying him apprehensively. 'You won't laugh?'

He had to smile; but with love and compassion. 'No.'

Princess Charlotte reached into the box and took out two tortoises, each with the royal coat of arms painted on its shell.

'No man, no woman, no husband, no wife,' she declared. 'have ever enjoyed so perfect a relationship.'

She waited for him to speak, hardly drawing a breath. Without effort he said: 'I believe you.'

'And you do like them both, don't you?'

'I think they're very handsome.'

She bent adoringly over her tortoises. 'That makes me so happy.' She stared at them, not looking round at Leopold. When she spoke, her stammer threatened to strangle every syllable. 'Y-y-you see . . . I th-thought you . . . you . . you'd think I was t-terribly . . .' She bit on a wavering breath. 'So childish. But these two ugly people are so silent . . . ugly . . . and so h-happy.' She was weeping. 'Do you understand, L-l-leop-p-p-'

'Charlotte.' His hand covered hers, over one of the tortoises. ' "Leo" is easier than "Leopold".'

'Leo?'

'Yes.'

'It's only when I'm worried,' she cried, 'and need to say what concerns me that I c-c-can't say . . . say . . . what I . . .'

'Want,' he supplied. He murmured at her, making it easy and loving. 'Perhaps I already know. After all, I have the letter you wrote me. A very beautiful letter. You may be surprised to learn I actually know it by heart.'

'I sh-shouldn't have — '

'Oh, but you should.'

'It was so b-brief. So . . . but so much what I wanted to *say* to you. I w-wanted . . . w-w-wanted to say . . .' She could go no further, could not speak at all.

The sight of her struggle moved him more deeply than he could ever have imagined possible. She must learn – he must teach her – that love was not so difficult, not so painful.

'I can think of no reason on this earth why I shouldn't say for you what you wished to say. Because you did, after all, write it; and I know it by heart. So I'll say, as you said: "Leopold, I'm inordinately fond of you so I shan't tell you." Well, Princess Charlotte, *I* am inordinately fond of *you*. And I shan't tell you.'

She cradled both tortoises in her left arm and put out her right hand for Leopold's, drawing it to her lips and kissing his knuckles hard.

Slowly but without hesitation she said: 'Your Royal Highness Prince Leopold of Saxe-Coburg-Saafeld, I am inordinately fond of you.'

He laughed, reached out for her, half expected the tortoises to bark or miaow or somehow protest. 'Perhaps,' he said, 'you'll now allow me to replace your beautiful sleeping royal tortoises? For Charlotte, I adore you. I would like to hold you in my arms. And for you to hold me in yours.'

They were married at Carlton House on 2nd May 1816. It was if anything an even more splendid occasion than the swearing-in of the Prince Regent five years earlier. The sun blazed in through the windows with their inset coats of arms, casting sparks of colour on a smiling assembly of dukes, duchesses, ambassadors, army and navy officers, and a phalanx of bishops. There were velvet cushions for royal knees, altar candlesticks taller than a man, and an octet of musicians well rehearsed in melodies formal and gay, religious and secular.

At the altar Prince Leopold waited in a dove-grey uniform with glittering orders, a number of them bestowed on him a couple of days before by the Prince Regent. With his skin-tight white pantaloons, dress sword and scabbard, and the tricorne hat under his arm, he was a picture of what a prince and a bridegroom should be. When the Prince Regent entered with Charlotte on his arm, he hesitated for a second and looked enviously at this picture of young manhood. Then he led his daughter, in a silver tinsel dress and with her hair wreathed in diamond roses, down the aisle formed between the assembled guests. Charlotte was radiant with happiness. When Leopold turned his head in silent welcome, his happiness answered hers. The Prince Regent unshamedly let the tears course down his cheeks; for he, too, was happy.

Leopold and his bride spent their honeymoon in the Duke of York's house at Oatlands in Surrey. Then, after a short spell in Park Lane, they moved into a country home provided by the Regent, and subsidized by an admiring and generous Parliament, at Claremont near Esher. In the house and its spacious grounds they were loving and merry, learning more about each other day and night, and marvelling at what they learned. Charlotte's hoydenish moments grew fewer, smoothed away by the sensitive and knowledgeable Leopold. And Leopold's own slight stiffness of manner was now leavened with laughter and a new, easy tolerance. They entertained groups of friends, but not lavishly and not too frequently: for weeks on end they were content to entertain their own two selves.

The Prince Regent was delighted. Leopold's strength of character surprised him; but won his respect. He could almost persuade himself that the marriage had from the start been exclusively his own idea. The pleasure he found in his daughter's happiness took away some of his own pains. His gout continued to plague him, and he had grown so fat that it required a special device to get him up on horseback. Both these matters were pounced on and savagely exploited by the caricaturists. But while he was still the butt of enemies and detractors, his daughter and her husband were the darlings of the nation; and for once the Prince was not jealous.

Ruefully he felt that Charlotte deserved this long-delayed contentment. Perhaps he had been too strict. And he had not been demonstrative enough when she was little and impressionable. Looking back, he had to confess that he had never played with her or sung silly songs or swung her about in his arms as he had done with Minnie Seymour. Dear little Minnie. But how unfair on Charlotte that he should have been so worried about any manifestation of her dreadful mother's influence that he had not thought of trying gentler ways with her.

Now all was well.

Within a very short time there were further grounds for rejoicing. It was soon known that the Princess Charlotte was with child.

Let it be a boy, prayed the Prince Regent. Let the succession be assured by a young prince. Someday, surely, his father must die at last and then he would cease to be Regent and at last become King. Then his dear daughter would be a worthy Queen of England, and must be followed by another prince, another King. Everything was going so incredibly well.

Some weeks before his grandchild was due, the Prince Regent went cheerfully off to a shooting party given by his friends the Hertfords on their Sudbourne estate in Suffolk. He expected to be back in time to welcome the next generation into the world; but had left instructions that should there be signs of an early delivery he must be summoned at once.

The summons came just after he had brought down four

fine pheasants in swift sequence, and was accepting a congratulatory glass of port from the servant at his elbow. One of Lord Hertford's grooms came hurrying along the ride behind them, bearing a letter for the Prince.

'News from Claremont?' Eagerly he opened it.

Your Royal Highness. May I beg you to return with all speed. My Princess Charlotte has been in the greatest pain. The labour has started but is very slow, and she complains of a singing in her mind. I fear, dear Sir, for her life and the child she carries. I beg you to hasten to us. Your obedient and loving Leopold.

Lord Hertford, horrified at what he read in the Prince's face, put out a hand to support him. Then he said:

'You need a carriage, sir?'

'At once.'

The Prince Regent left in the clothes he had been wearing for the shoot, cold in spite of their warmth, cold with a dread such as he had never in his life experienced. He shouted at the postillions, and the horses were urged on and on. There was no time for a change of horses; no time for anything but a wild gallop through hour upon terrible hour. Other coaches lurched to one side to make way. Once the Prince saw a man on horseback galloping even more feverishly in the direction from which they had come; but there was no way of knowing whether he carried tidings of the Princess, or of calling him back to make sure.

'Please God,' the Prince was intoning desperately, 'assist my love, my daughter. Help her, God. Please help me, and help her. Dear God . . . .'

They thundered on.

It was night when at last the panting, lathered horses stumbled to a halt outside the portico of Claremont. The Prince was out of the carriage before any groom or footman could reach the door or attempt to help him down. He burst through the hall, to find Leopold standing at the top of the staircase.

'My dear boy, how are you?' The Prince clutched the balustrade and went up two steps, three steps. His prayers had been answered. They must have been answered. He had been a fool to take fright. All would be well. 'Am I a grandfather?' he said. 'Are you a father? And how is our dear Charlotte?'

Leopold stumbled down towards him, a faltering step at a time; and took his father-in-law in his arms. 'Dear beloved man.'

'The news!'

'I love her.'

'Yes. And the child?'

'A son.'

'A son!' cried the Prince Regent.

'Born dead.' Leopold's arms tightened around those plump, flabby shoulders which were beginning to quiver uncontrollably.

'And my daughter . . . your wife . . .?'

'Oh, Christ Jesus.'

'No.' The Prince pushed it back, away, far from him.

'She died in great pain.' Leopold fought off the Prince's despair. 'In great pain and . . . oh, God . . . great dignity. Like her own features, our son's features were quite still – and perfect.'

'It is a nightmare,' said the Prince. 'None of this is true.'

Leopold did not let him go. 'Her last words were, "Leopold, I have tried to love you as you deserve." And then, with that hesitation – that adorable stammer, that hesitation – she said as clearly as a tiny bell, like a little chiming bell, she said, "And tell my father he is the most beautiful of God's creatures. And that I knew him and loved him. Cherish him, Leopold, because his subjects do not. But he will live in their memory. Above all, be sure to tell him how I loved him." And I held her in my arms, and it was at an end.'

It could not be true; but was true. Like all the fleeting happinesses at which the Prince of Wales had so ardently grasped, it had cheated him.

There would be no Queen Charlotte on the throne of England. And there would be no grandson of George Augustus Frederick, Prince Regent, to follow her as true Hanoverian inheritor of the realm.

CHAPTER SIX

When it was clear that the Prince Regent was unlikely to set himself the task of supplying another legitimate heir to the throne, it dawned on his brothers and sisters that they, too, were sadly lacking in legitimate offspring. The five girls were spinsters or childless. Some of George's brothers had been keeping mistresses for years and producing a number of bastards: William, Duke of Clarence, had sired ten. But now William and the other Royal Dukes who had so far been content with unwedded bliss must, in middle age, look around for suitable wives, and work to secure the future of the dynasty.

The likeliest candidate for this crucial fatherhood was the Duke of Kent, who was urged by the newspapers to bring to an end his twenty-seven years of happiness with Madame de St Laurent and seek out a European princess. Within a few months he selected Prince Leopold's widowed sister Victoria, who had proved her ability to function as required by conceiving two children in her first marriage; and obliged her new husband and the nation by giving birth to a daughter within a year of the second marriage.

The child's godfather must beyond question be the Prince Regent, and naturally she must be given the name Georgiana.

The Duke and Duchess of Kent presented their daughter for christening in the Cupola Room at Kensington Palace. At the last moment the Prince complained that they were providing too many names for the child and in any case had got them all in the wrong order. Georgiana Charlotte Augusta Alexandrina Victoria simply would not do. He could not by protocol allow a version of his own name to precede that of the Tsar, so Alexandrina should come first.

But he was equally unwilling to take second place, and therefore it would be best to drop Georgiana altogether. As for Charlotte, he was appalled at their callousness in using the name of his dear dead daughter.

No final decision had been reached when the Archbishop of Canterbury stood before the Duchess of Kent, with the wailing infant in her arms, and addressed the godfather.

'Dost thou, in the name of this child, renounce the Devil and all his works, the vain pomp and glory of the world, with all covetous desires of the flesh, so that thou wilt not follow nor be led by them?'

'I renounce them all,' affirmed the Prince with the greatest conviction.

'Dost thou believe in God the Father Almighty, maker of Heaven and Earth . . .'

Five names, thought the Prince, was indubitably too many. He must make a choice, and not mind what these other dunderheads thought. But really, such unpromising material! As the Archbishop rambled on to a counterpoint of the baby's squawling, a certain dizziness began to afflict the Regent. He wished to be out of here, to be done with it. What right had this deplorably noisy, messy little lump of flesh to inherit all that he had so painstakingly built up? Why should he, in the course of time, have to step down and be no more, while this insignificant scrap of humanity had the world before her?

'. . . and the everlasting life after death?'

'All this,' said the Prince resoundingly. 'I steadfastly believe.'

The Archbishop took the child from her mother's arms and, cradling her, said to the Prince:

'Name this child.'

The Duke and Duchess of Kent stared imploringly.

The Prince said: 'Alexandrina.'

They mutely begged that he should go on. Let him reshuffle the names as he chose, but let them come out in some reasonable order.

There was a terrible pause. The Archbishop looked down with reverent distaste at the damp bundle in his arms, and awaited the royal decree.

The Duke leaned forward to prompt his brother. 'Augusta.'

The Prince Regent started. Augusta sounded far too grand, he decided. He looked at the tearful face of the far from enticing Duchess, and said irascibly: 'Oh, let her be called after her mother.' And as the Archbishop still waited for the definite pronouncement, he thundered: 'Alexandrina *Victoria*.'

'Alexandrina Victoria,' the Archbishop thankfully echoed, 'I baptize thee in the name of the Father, and of the Son, and of the Holy Ghost. Amen.'

'Amen,' sobbed the Duchess of Kent.

The child soon took a toddling step closer to the throne. Queen Charlotte had died the year after her granddaughter Princess Charlotte's death. The Duke of York had taken over her duties as guardian of his mad father; and was at Windsor on that January day in 1820 when at last King George III died.

The 'high and mighty Prince, George, Prince of Wales' was Regent no longer, but King George IV.

'Long live the King,' chanted the crowds after the proclamation, with no great fervour. And then, with much greater enthusiasm: 'And long live the Queen.'

The fret of it had always been there at the back of George's mind. Now it came urgently to the forefront. There was no avoiding the issue. In all prayers offered by clergy throughout the land for the new monarch, the Queen was also prayed for by name. George called his religious and political advisers to him and ordered the deletion of all such references from all prayers and ceremonies. He also insisted that during preparations for the Coronation, no room must be left for Caroline and no mention of her must creep into the service. And under no circumstances must she return to England.

There was just a slender hope that she might in any case not wish to come back. All the reports said that she had been enjoying her freedom in Europe: had, indeed, enjoyed it so unabashedly that all her original household had deserted her and she now consorted with a succession of musicians, dissolute young officers, and an Italian adventurer named Pergami. This latest conquest was seen everywhere with her in public, and servants eagerly reported on what they did in private. On one occasion in Genoa, Pergami rode in style before a phaeton decorated to represent a sea-shell and driven by a child in flesh-coloured tights, while the fifty-year-old Caroline sprawled back in a low-cut pink bodice and short skirt, making a great display of her plump legs. On other occasions there were tales of noisy passion in a tent aboard ship, and drunken revels in a score of Italian towns and villages.

Nobody had officially notified Caroline of her daughter's death. When she wept at the belatedly delivered news, she had her gallants to console her, and seemed easy enough to console; though there were those who said that if she ever set foot in England again she would wreak a dreadful revenge on the heartless ones.

The King clamoured for a speedy divorce. His counsellors blenched. A formal divorce action would allow Caroline to speak out publicly in her own defence: and how, in such circumstances, could the names of Mrs Fitzherbert, Lady Jersey and a dozen others not be bandied about to the detriment of the King and his cause?

For the time being let her at least be kept out of the country, and kept quiet.

Lord Malmesbury, retired and with only a short time to live, was no longer the inevitable diplomatic confidant. Even if he had still been active, the King might have frowned on his being sent on any mission to Caroline. Was it not Harris who had been responsible for bringing that appalling creature into the country in the first place, without uttering a single warning to her prospective bridegroom of what was in store for him? In present circumstances the Government thought it wise to approach Henry Brougham with a view to his acting as confidential emissary to the absent Princess who was now nominally Queen. Could it be discreetly put to her that she should, in return for a reasonable financial consideration, remain abroad and agree not to assume the style and title of Queen of England but be content with some lesser but valid title such as, perhaps, Duchess of Cornwall? The figure of fifty thousand pounds a year was suggested.

The King was not greatly enamoured of Brougham, either. The scheming lawyer had adopted extreme Whiggish views in Parliament, condemned the Prince Regent's closeness to the Tory Hertfords, and openly declared himself a friend of Caroline's. But it was this friendship which the Government hoped to use in reaching a cautious settlement.

Brougham set off.

Caroline received him in the drawing-room of a château she had leased near St Omer. She showed every sign of pleasure. Brougham had spoken up on her behalf before now, and she was sure he had come to smooth her path back to England and her rightful place on the throne.

When he had explained his mission, her pleasure faded, while her colour intensified. Two brighter red spots appeared in her already fiery, raddled cheeks. When he continued with a disquisition on the advantages which would accrue if she fell in with the Government's generous offer, she suddenly erupted into the middle of his pleading.

'Mister Brougham, I am not a whore to be purchased by the British Government. I am Queen of England.'

'Ma'am, as I've tried to make clear — '

'You make it clear that I am offered fifty thousand pounds to deny the truth. To stay out of your country, pretend I have no title connecting me with the royal family, and never visit Britain or any of her dominions. But you make up my mind for me. I will visit Britain. I will return to the English people, who love me.'

'Dear lady, I entreat you once more to reflect upon the step you wish to take.'

'Step?' she cried. 'Step, Mr Brougham? I will swim the Channel if needs be. The people hate my husband and hate their oppressors. They adore me, they will want me there – so I shall be there.'

'Your Royal Highness — '

'Should it not be "Your Majesty"?'

'Your Majesty, I have endeavoured to be a faithful counsel to you these many years,' said Brougham sombrely. 'I trust I may continue to be so trusted. But while I know some of your supporters feed you with assurances that you have only to return to be rapturously received, I do feel you should be more circumspect. I promise that I'm ready to negotiate on your behalf terms with the Government whereby your annuity may perhaps be granted even without renunciation of rank or title or right. You may also, just possibly, be received by diplomatic agents abroad. Your Majesty need not court the favour of certain elements among the British people like some parliamentary candidate at an election. It's not denied that you are Queen of England. All that is asked is that you shall not assert your rights in such a way as to threaten the peace of the realm. Any direct appeal or exhibition will be hurtful to your Majesty's dignity.'

She was fat and red-faced, and smelled little more savoury than when the Prince of Wales had first recoiled from her. But there was a certain splendour in her manner which cowed even the icy, calculating Brougham: a flourish which had from the start endeared her to him even when his primary concern had been for his own advancement. She said resolutely:

'As for dignity, your King has little of it, and your law-givers are detested. The rank and file will be with me. In the past, Mister Brougham, you have declared yourself my virtual Attorney-General. Your friend Denman might, then be my Solictor-General? You will act on my behalf?'

'That was not my purpose in coming here,' Brougham protested.

'Will you stand by me or will you not?'

Brougham wilted. Then he said: 'Indeed I will, your Majesty. But you must understand this may be not just one battle with one simple outcome. We may be launching a war.'

'A war of words,' said Caroline. Obviously the idea stimulated her. 'That does not frighten me – or you?'

'No, it does not frighten me.'

'Very well, then. We will make this war of words together, for the sake of the British people. I shall return to England.'

'So be it,' said Brougham, valiant but appalled.

In 5th June 1820 Caroline landed at Dover, plump and resplendent in an ermine-lined puce pelisse and a white Leghorn hat. An enthusiastic rabble thronged round her and insisted on drawing her carriage through the streets to her hotel. When she set out for London there were welcoming groups at every crossroads and in every village street. Word raced ahead and brought her admirers out on the approaches to the capital, until there was scarcely an unoccupied inch between Greenwich and Westminster Bridge. She was accompanied in an open landau by Alderman Wood, the latest entrepreneur to espouse her cause. He looked much more pompous and much duller than the discarded Pergami; but this was to some extent compensated for by a following carriage in which sat several of Caroline's other Italian associates and the inevitable Willikin. Alderman Wood had the honour of lodging his Queen in his home in South Audley Street. In the wake of their triumphal progress, crowds exuberantly smashed in the windows of known antagonists and then went on a rampage, attacking the Duke of Wellington's carriage, stoning Lord Sidmouth's house, smashing in the windows of

Lady Hertford's home, and storming around Carlton House.

She should not have been allowed to reach England; yet had reached it. She was Queen; yet must under no circumstances continue to be so. How could she be halted?

CHAPTER SEVEN

King George IV sat in his library in his Brighton Pavilion and despaired. He and Nash had laboured so long to create this magnificent setting for a magnificent Regency and now an incomparable Monarchy. The wind was set fair for the triumph of good taste and aesthetic values over vulgar makeshift. But a cloud had drifted across the Channel and was darkening Brighton, the south coast, and the capital itself.

Lord Liverpool, whose administration had survived far beyond anyone's most sanguine expectations, sat respectfully awaiting the royal command. To either side he had the Duke of York, the Lord Chancellor, the King's Attorney-General and Solicitor-General, and the King's infallible aide and sycophant, Colonel McMahon.

The King stated his case forthrightly. 'Gentlemen, to clear the air of any hypocrisy I will state baldly that the issue is this: sexual intercourse with the Queen of England.' He saw them tense, and went unrelentingly on. 'I am bound to say that no sane man would copulate with that accursed harridan. But there is evidence that some wretches have done so. A wealth of evidence. And violation of the King's wife is tantamount to high treason. Yet I am informed that no action can be taken against this presumptuous Italian, this Pergami. I, the King of England, cannot bring to justice the braggart who has made a mockery of my marriage. Is this so?'

'Your Majesty,' said Lord Liverpool, 'the fornicator Pergami is a foreigner. The adulterous connection was achieved on foreign soil.'

'My ancestors have gone to war for less than this.'

'The Italian's actions are beyond the province of English

law. Treason is therefore not relevant. However, the House of Lords is fully aware of evidence that the Queen's conduct has been of the most licentious iniquity, and disturbs the moral feeling and honour of the entire country.'

'Then if we can't get her paramour into our courts, can't we at least make *her* the subject of some solemn public inquiry, so that the entire country, as you put it, may see the truth?'

Liverpool said: 'I have in mind the introduction of a Bill of Pains and Penalties. Under this device the conduct of the Italian and others may be judicially examined and shown to be licentious, degrading and adulterous. It is no troublesome divorce action, your Majesty, but a procedure whose findings should make it possible by straightforward Act of Parliament to disown the Queen and deprive her of her title. At the same time, once the evidence has been proven, it can be decreed that your Majesty's marriage shall for ever be wholly dissolved, annulled, and made void. To save the indecency and inconvenience of two parliamentary hearings, I shall rule that the matter be left to the House of Lords alone, and the Commons then asked simply for ratification.'

The King nodded. Liverpool was continuing to display unexpected capabilities. 'I leave this whole distasteful affair in your hands,' he said graciously. 'But take good care that they do not fumble.'

The public was enraged. Although proceedings were being instituted at the behest of Parliament, no one had any doubt but that George their King was behind the whole business. And how dared he, of all men, raise such hypocritical protests? What of the royal dallyings with Mrs Fitzherbert, with Lady Jersey and Lady Hertford and Lady Bessborough; and now, even while accusing his Queen of immorality, what of his diversions with the fat and fawning grandmother, Lady Conyngham? In the towns and cities there were protests. Some authorities feared that revolution was in the air.

Mr George Canning resigned, declaring he did so as a matter of pure principle, rather than be a party to governmental proceedings against Queen Caroline.

Nevertheless on 5th July 1820 Lord Liverpool brought in his

> Bill entitled an Act to deprive Her Majesty, Caroline Amelia Elizabeth, of the Titles, Prerogatives, Rights, Privileges and Exemptions, of Queen Consort of this Realm, and to dissolve the Marriage between His Majesty and the said Caroline Amelia Elizabeth.

Although the preliminary inquiry was nominally a Parliamentary matter and not a civil or criminal trial, the world knew that in effect Queen Caroline was on trial. For the second reading of the Bill and the subsequent investigatory procedure it was conceded that Caroline might be represented by counsel and, though forbidden to speak in her own defence, could attend the hearings in the House of Lords.

By the time the day came, the Queen and her supporters had whipped up the enthusiasm of the mob again, and there were roars of cheering as she arrived at the House in a richly appointed six-horse coach. She was attired in black gauze with lacy trimmings and chaste white sleeves – the black in deference to the recently deceased Duchess of York. Some of the dignity was unfortunately offset by her wig of greasy black ringlets and her charcoal-black eyebrows. But as she approached the door and asked for admittance, her bearing over-awed Sir Thomas Tyrwhitt, in his official garb as Black Rod, and instead of treating her as offhandedly as had been suggested to him he acknowledged her as Queen and escorted her to the gilt and scarlet chair provided for her. When it was noticed how dumpy and short-legged she was, a footstool was brought also.

Temporary galleries had been set up about the walls so that members of the House of Commons could stroll through and divert themselves with snatches of the proceedings. Below, benches for the peers were built up in three tiers to each side of the House, covered in scarlet cloth.

The Lord Chancellor, Lord Eldon, was established on a crimson velvet stool at the table of the House so that he could take notes. To either side of him sat a Chief Justice, and beyond them the further complement of seven judges.

When the clerk had called the roll of Lords Spiritual and Temporal there came a single, ominous clap of thunder above the roof of the building. To both sides, prosecution and defence, it was an omen they longed to interpret in their own favour.

Not until the third day of depositions and formal procedure did the Lord Chancellor call upon the Attorney-General to open his case.

Sir Robert Gifford, who had been occupying a large part of these days in rehearsing phrases for the hundredth time and reshuffling papers in case he had missed the opportunity of scoring a good opening shot, rose to his feet and moved to the bar of the House.

'My Lords. I have, my Lords, to state the circumstances which are to be adduced in evidence to your Lordships in support of those heavy and serious charges made in the preamble of the Bill: charges which reflect not only the greatest scandal and disgrace upon the individual against whom they are made but also the greatest disgrace against the country itself.' Relishing the cadences of his own vocal chords, he raised the pitch for the benefit of his audience. 'The highest individual, as a subject, in the country is charged with one of the most serious offences against the laws of both God and man: it is that of adulterous intercourse.' He paused dramatically so that the echoes might settle. 'Silence can no longer be observed. And my noble listeners must be warned that this painful narrative is filled with scenes so disgusting as to offend every regulated mind.'

Henry Brougham let out a long, resonant growl. Gifford turned a fine glare upon him. So strict was it that Caroline's defendant knew he must apologize or lose a point before he had even entered the lists.

Reluctantly he offered: 'I did not mean to interrupt the learned person.'

Gifford allowed himself a stately, unforgiving bow. Then he resumed his peroration.

'Some time in October 1814, Her Majesty engaged one Bartolomeo Pergami as courier, or footman, or *valet de place*, in Milan. When the household translated itself to Naples it was observed that the said Pergami, through the pleasure of Her Majesty, was provided with a bedroom adjacent to Her Majesty's. The suspicions of a female servant were excited on the morning of 9th November when it was clear that Her Majesty had not slept in her bed but in that of Pergami's. I submit that there will be evidence before your Lordships that there were decisive marks on the bed sheets of two people having' – he allowed himself a breath and a tremor of hesitation – '*slept* between them. The following morning, some persons of distinction were led to present their respects to Her Majesty, but she proved accessible to none of them. This was the commencement of that most scandalous, degrading, most licentious intercourse which continued and increased. The natural effect was to lessen the distance which must exist between persons of royal rank and menial servants. Pergami thenceforth became more haughty and took on an air of greater importance, which grew as the intercourse proceeded. Some days later, Her Majesty was dressed for a masked ball by Pergami. She appeared as the Genius of History. The dress was extremely indecent and disgusting, and Pergami assisted her into it. That same night a servant heard noises of Her Majesty's intimacies with Pergami. They were those of degrading intercourse. And, your Lordships will be bound to observe Pergami was and is married to another, and thus a *double* adulterer. His intercourse with Her Majesty continued daily and with scarce an interruption.'

The accusations droned on. Brougham ventured a reassuring smile at the Queen, who shuffled her shoes on the footstool but continued to stare contemptuously ahead through the mesh of her veil.

Gifford reached other climes and events. 'After travelling in Italy and Switzerland until November 1815. Her Majesty went by boat to Sicily and thence to Tunis. She conferred upon Pergami the dignity of a Knight of Malta and always addressed him as "Chevalier", and made him Chamberlain, adding the title of Baron della Francia and the Order of Saint Sepulchre. Not content with this, she instituted an order of her own – the Order of Saint Caroline – and conferred it on innumerable servants and finally created Pergami the Grand Master.'

There was a roar of laughter throughout the House.

Gifford made the most of it. 'Smile, your Lordships, smile. But it indicates the powerful influence of adulterous intercourse over Her Majesty.'

The hours went by. Another day dawned. Gifford, refreshing himself with a medicinal water to ease his thickening throat, proceeded with his denunciation.

'Her Majesty now embarked at Jaffa for Italy on board a polacca. She had a tent erected on the deck with a bed for herself and, your Lordships, a sofa for Pergami. Intercourse was thus maintained for a very considerable time indeed inside the tent. She had a bath prepared for her. Pergami attended the ablutions. It will be observed that the nature of this disgusting intercourse was inflamed by a theatrical performance held later, upon the return of Her Majesty to Italy. There were several performances by one Mahomet – imitations, in the most indelicate manner, of sexual intercourse. They were not merely indecent' – the Attorney-General indulged himself in a whirlwind of outrage – 'but of *disgusting* indecency.'

The outline of the attack was clarifying. Now it remained only for the earnest prosecutor to fill in the details for which the House of Lords and the newspaper and print sellers had been pruriently waiting. Two days after the opening of his narration, Sir Robert began calling witnesses.

When Theodore Majocci, most elegantly attired, minced across the floor of the House, Queen Caroline raised her veil and then let out a sob of anguish.

'Theodore! Oh, no . . . no!'

Her attendant escorted her away. The assembled judges and noble jurors might make what they chose of this.

Gifford said: 'As a friend of Pergami's, and subsequently as a livery servant, you travelled with Her Majesty and Pergami in a carriage to Italy. Do you remember in your preparation of the carriage finding a bottle in it?'

'I do.'

'Answer "yes" or "no",' said Gifford pedantically.

'Yes.' Majocci was eager to please.

'And was the opening or mouth of the bottle four inches in diameter?'

'Yes.'

'From what you found from time to time in the bottle, for what was it used?'

'For Pergami to pass water into.'

Henry Brougham was on his feet. 'Irrelevant.'

There were cries of 'Order, order!'

'Do you recall any time,' Gifford demanded, 'at which Her Majesty was present at an exhibition of the dance provided by a Mr Mahomet?'

'I do. Yes.'

'And what did Mr Mahomet do?'

'He perform a *giucco*.'

'Which is what?'

'A trick.'

'Perhaps you would stand on the table and show their Lordships the exact nature of this trick.'

Majocci looked doubtful, but there were willing hands to

help him on to the table. He stared around. A heavier doubt began to afflict him.

'Go on,' urged Gifford.

Majocci pulled open the front of his pantaloons. There was a ripple of sniggering along the tiers of noble gentlemen, and then an expectant hush. Majocci's doubts vanished. Acting and over-acting, he reached within his pantaloons and pulled out the tail of his shirt, waggling it up and down. The sniggers exploded into unashamed laughter.

'Very well,' said Gifford. 'Your Lordships may make of that what they will.'

'It's a form of Eastern curtsy,' Brougham attempted.

That was a mistake. The laughter ran for a moment out of control. Gifford allowed it to follow its course while Majocci was helped down from the table, and then said:

'My Lords, that is all I have at the present moment to ask this witness.'

Brougham allowed no interval for muttering and speculation. He moved in sharply with: 'I trust, my Lords, I shall now be permitted to enter upon the cross-examination of this witness. I am ready to do so.'

Majocci, rather pleased with the reaction to his impromptu exhibition, was disconcerted by this new inquisitor's tone of voice. It would have been more appropriate for him to be allowed to leave, dancing out to the accompaniment of hilarious applause. Instead, the House was silent once more save for this freezing voice.

Brougham faced him. 'There was no way at all aboard the polacca that Pergami could have gone to Her Majesty's bed without interrupting the sleep of not one but at least two servants?'

Majocci stared. His earlier fluency had deserted him. The readiness to answer had dried up. Trying to work out the deeper meaning of the question, he played for time:

'Non mi ricordo.'

'You mean you don't know?'

'Non mi ricordo.'

'You don't recall?'

'Non mi ricordi questo.'

'But you, Mr Majocci, were one of those servants,' said Brougham furiously. 'And you dare to say you don't recall?'

Majocci flinched. *'Non mi ricordi questo.'*

'Consider this black performer, Mahomet, if you will. It was merely one part of a performance, a long obscure comedy, in which the performer showed his shirt tail as a comic fellow – briefly?'

'Non mi ricordo.'

'You mean you don't recall Mahomet, in spite of your convincing impersonation?'

'Si,' said Majocci, shaking. *'Si.* Yes. I mean, no.'

Protest and derision surged up around the chamber.

Brougham cut through it. 'Do you recall – *ricordo* – receiving a visit at the Villa Villani from a German baron, one Baron Ompteda?'

Whether the question was clear to him or not, Majocci clearly recognized the name. Desperately he blustered back: *'Non mi ricordo.'*

'And this Baron Ompteda offered you money to visit England and give evidence here today?'

Majocci tried to control his distress. 'I remember to have received no money when I arrive at Milan. *Ricordo di no, mi ricordo che no.* I remember I did not – non so, I do not know, *più no che si,* more no than yes.' He struck his left temple. *'Non mi ricordo!'*

'My Lords,' said Brougham haughtily, 'I have done with this witness. I have no further questions to ask of him. In a common case I should certainly be satisfied with this examination. In this present case I have certainly no reason to ask him a single question further.'

Nor, said his contemptuous eyebrows, should anyone here present today think there was any point in asking any further questions or expecting anything better from any prosecution witness.

The days came and went. The witnesses came and went. There were men who had stooped to peer through key-holes, men who had listened to the noises made by a man and a woman in heat, servants who had been obsequious to one mistress and were now willing to further the aims of another master.

'Did you ever see Pergami do anything jocular?'

'*Si.*' There was a sly, ready, responsive laugh. 'I see him once put some cushions under Her Majesty's Grecian robe. To make her laugh.'

'An innocent trick?'

'To make Her Royal Highness laugh, *si.*'

'That is no answer.'

'Meaning that it is not the answer,' Brougham interjected frigidly, 'which my learned friend wants.'

And then there was the servant Cuchi.

'Where were you placed when you saw Pergami and Her Majesty in each other's clothes?'

'I was stooped.'

'Why?'

'My eye was at the key-hole.'

Laughter in the House clashed with indignant cries for order. Farce mingled with fury.

'And Pergami's hand was where?'

'Upon the part of Her Majesty.'

'And Her Majesty's hand?'

'Upon the part of Pergami.'

Slowly the picture was assembled, or reassembled like a wall painting from ancient times put together from torn and splintered fragments. But as it took shape again it was no masterpiece: the lines and colours and theme were stained and ugly.

At last the work of restoration was complete. The procession of inept, laughable, sly, clumsy, eager and evasive witnesses came to an end. Queen Caroline, who had started out in fine defiant fettle, became progressively more dejected – largely, some observers felt, from the eagerness of her own retainers to sell her secrets for ready money and, indeed, to invent when required.

The Attorney-General had told his rapt listeners what to expect, and the witnesses had lived up to expectations. Now Henry Brougham stood by the bar of the House to persuade them that they had misinterpreted every scene painted by these witnesses.

'I am borne up in my task,' he averred, 'by the knowledge of the conviction of this assembly's justice, and by the innocence of my client. By the knowledge of the innocence of my illustrious client – a knowledge shared, your Lordships, with all mankind.' Brougham paused, and offered the serried ranks of peers a wry, dismissive smile. 'I grant that Her Majesty left for Italy and moved in a society very different from what she had known in this country, and probably inferior.' Like a finely attuned actor he allowed for the laughter. 'Yet whilst Her Majesty was in England she threw open her doors to the peers of England and their families. She received them, and was received by them. But then, abroad? Abroad, she was reduced to the alternative of begging society for its favour. She received no friendly communication from her family. She received no invitation to the wedding of her beloved daughter, and no notification of the death of that daughter. If she sought different company, was she not justified in doing so?'

He told the story which had already been told, but with different emphasis. When there was a snort of derision, he stared the perpetrator down. When a bishop leaned forward to whisper to a marquess, he stopped speaking as if in deference, until the colloquy dissolved into embarrassed silence.

'A masquerade was held at a theatre, I believe called the Theatre of Saint Charles. To this Her Majesty rose up to go with her companions, dressed, according to the evidence of one witness, in 'a most indecent and disgusting dress'. And when pressed for a description of it, this witness said she wore a mask. Strange as it may seem to your Lordships, Her Majesty wore a mask at a masquerade! One might say that if she had not worn a mask she would have had no business there.'

Laughter carried him on at some moments, slowed his pace at others. But he had the House in his grip and would not let them escape.

'And the witnesses, this miserable army of servants? They have thrown discretion and trust to the winds. They appear from their own testimony to have given themselves up to the base gratifications of prurient peep-holing. And yet, when questioned, there was invariably not *one* peeper present to see a lady's arm actually round a man's neck, not *three*; nay, not *four*; but invariably *eleven* or *twelve*. My colleagues the Attorney-General and Solicitor-General maintain that all acts of such privacy were carried out in the public gaze. Every movement is described in detail – the adjustment of a dress, the passing of water in a bottle, the stains on sheets, any number of kisses, the noise of the act of intercourse itself – all carried out before an army of witnesses. Was such folly ever known in the history of human acts? Was ever such folly so extravagantly disclosed in the most unthinking acts even of that youthful period when the blood boils in the veins?' Brougham drew a deep breath and suddenly shouted up into the rafters: 'It speaks of reckless insanity.'

He continued to unravel the threads of testimony and show them in new colours. Ridiculing each witness and drowning every sentence of the evidence in scorn, he provoked a number of admiring nods – for his oratory if not for his accuracy.

At last, very quietly, he said: 'My Lords, I call upon you to pause. You stand on the brink of a precipice. Save the country. Save yourselves. Rescue the country. Save the people of whom you are the ornaments, but severed from whom you can no more live than the blossom that is severed from the root and tree on which it grows. Save the Crown! Save the altar! You see that when the church and the throne would allow of no church solemnity on behalf of the Queen, by erasing her name from the Liturgy, the heartfelt prayers of the people rose to Heaven for her protection. I pray Heaven for her. I here pour forth my fervent supplications at the throne of mercy, that mercies may descend on the people of this country richer than their rulers have deserved.' He paused, and concluded heavily: 'And that your hearts may be turned to justice.'

For a long minute he stayed where he was at the bar; then stepped back and slumped down into his chair. As a congratulatory murmur ran round the peers' benches, he raised his head and looked to one side for the Queen's approval.

Her chair was empty.

'Where is the Queen?' he whispered to Denham, who was leaning forward to shake his hand. 'I wished her to hear that.'

'She has sought some rest at her house.' Denman kept his voice low. 'With one of her Italians, I believe.'

'Let us pray God she keeps the curtains drawn.'

Another day, and another attack. But this time it was launched by the defence. Brougham had briefed a young barrister with meaning questions about the reliability of some witnesses and the absence of others. Where was the supposed villain of the piece, Pergami? Let the Solicitor-General produce him if he dared. And then, before it could be protested that there were no legal means for compelling Pergami to appear in England, it was quickly suggested that if he were produced at the bar he would simply (and, it went without saying, truthfully) deny the charges.

'This case, my Lords, is founded and bottomed on perjury!'

That was the defence's main theme. Respectable witnesses were presented to declare that the Eastern jokes and dances of which so much had been made were normal in those parts of the world and free from any salaciousness. A prim lady-in-waiting affirmed that Queen Caroline's easy manner with her servants was neither unusual nor disreputable. Young naval officers who had formed the Queen's bodyguard during some of her travels were summoned to say what they had seen and heard, to find whether this tallied with what the Italians had testified.

'Lieutenant Hownam, you are an officer in His Majesty's Royal Navy?'

'I am, sir.'

'Did you ever see Pergami commit adulterous intercourse with Her Majesty?'

'I did not, sir.'

'And, Lieutenant Hownam, is it your considered view that at night aboard the polacca, of which we have heard so much and in such lurid detail . . . no, let me put it differently . . . did you at any time hear noises?'

'Of what, sir?'

'From the tent on deck. After all, if I may explain to the House, you were in a position to *hear* what went on in the dark, were you not?'

'I understand, sir. Yes, I was able to hear noises.'

'What kind of noises?'

'From the animals in the hold.'

'On several occasions these prompted much laughter and jocularity, did they not? Please explain why.'

The young lieutenant looked awkwardly along the expectant faces of a row of peers, and shuffled his feet in embarrassment. 'They were of a . . . a singular nature, sir.'

'Explain!' The cry came from all sides.

'Mr Williams,' the Lord Chancellor instructed, 'you must ask the witness to explain himself.'

'I am a poor sort of actor, sir.'

'Go on, Lieutenant Hownam.'

The luckless Hownam took a shaky breath and then

emitted a loud mooing noise; and then, crimson in the face, the sound of an explosive fart.

The House adjourned in happy uproar.

For nigh on eleven weeks the inquiry dragged along its tortuous way. At last the Queen's own Solicitor-General, Denman, rose to sum up the case for the defence. In demanding an acquittal, he made the most of his opportunities for resounding phrases and declamations. It was a bravura performance, but there were moments when Brougham was observed to frown and look apprehensive. His own opening address for the defence had won many allies. He hoped Denman was not going to stumble and lose some of them.

'Is Her Majesty guilty of an unparallelled infringement of Royal authority?' Denman was challenging. 'Was it a crime, when Her Majesty visited the Holy Sepulchre, to do as the Dukes of Orléans and Bourbon had done before her, to institute an order of knighthood to reward those who accompanied her on the visit? Are you, my Lords, finally, definitely, certain without doubt, that you have been presented with evidence which incontrovertibly proves that the most licentious, disgusting and unforgivable adulterous sexual intercourse repeatedly took place? Has one single witness said that the infamous act was observed in all its details? No, no, no. And no!'

Denman conveniently glossed over the fact that among those rewarded with a knighthood in Caroline's order at Jerusalem had been the likeable young lieutenant who had spoken so convincingly in her defence.

'Where is the final proof of adultery? Where is the *corpus delicti*? My Lords, you have heard from one witness of the position of the hands of Pergami and Her Majesty upon their respective parts most private. My learned colleagues, under the direction of Sir Robert Gifford, have endeavoured to establish the most disgraceful facts that ever polluted the lips of man. My learned colleagues have dragged in the contents of ransacked filthy clothes bags;

they have raked through every sewer, pried into every water-closet, collected sheets they claim stained by lovers. This foulest of pursuits has led where? It has led to the misery of Her Majesty . . . and yet, still, the act is not proven. Did it or did it not occur? I crave the indulgence of every man of conscience here present to answer, from the depths of his heart, "Yes, it did," or, "No, no, no – I have not heard the proof".' Denman paused dramatically and then thundered: " 'I have not heard the *proof*!" '

Denman took ten hours over his speech, and concluded with a poetic fervour which made Brougham wince:

'If your Lordships have been furnished with powers, scarce possessed by Omniscience itself, to arrive at the secrets of this female, you will think it your duty to imitate the justice, beneficence, and wisdom of that benignant Being who, when guilt was detected and vice revealed, said: "If no accuser can come forward to condemn thee, neither do I condemn thee. Go, and sin no more." '

He sat down, exhausted, and glanced at Brougham for approval.

White-faced, Brougham said: 'Dear me, dear me. "Go and sin no more . . . !" Oh, dear me.'

'Did I go too far?' said Denham anxiously.

'My dear fellow, all along we have been maintaining that she *never* sinned. Your inference was that the Royal wrist be slapped and she should never again do whatever it was we said she didn't do in the first place. No matter. I believe we have proved her innocent in the eyes of the law. And that's all that counts.'

CHAPTER EIGHT

They brought the news with great trepidation from London to the King at Brighton. On 6th November the House of Lords, solemnly considering the evidence laid before it, had given the Bill a second reading and by a majority of twenty-eight agreed that the Queen was guilty. But then, at the third reading which should have carried it through for presentation to the House of Commons, the majority had dropped to nine. This was too close-run a thing. The Commons, alarmed by the unrest of the populace, and dubious about the whole archaic procedure of this Bill of Pains and Penalties, would almost certainly reject anything with such inconclusive backing from above.

The verdict of the Lords remained, in effect, 'Guilty'; but Lord Liverpool decreed that the Bill should be dropped.

The King was in a state of near-apoplexy.

But if the Queen had her followers, there were many whose study of the full debate left them with little doubt of Caroline's guilt. She had been exculpated not for reasons of innocence but because of political jousting. And if the mob revelled in scurrilous prints and broadsheets condemning the King, the King's supporters were ready to answer back in kind. Denunciations of the Queen in the form of obscene and farcical verses circulated almost as fast as caricatures of Lady Conyngham sprawling on the King's plump knees. And a jingle provoked by Denman's unfortunate phrasing began to go the round of the clubs:

Most gracious Queen, we thee implore
To go away and sin no more;
Or if that effort be too great,
Do go away at any rate.

All of which was entertaining for society and the mob; and some of which, according to its tenor, brought a vengeful smile to the King's face. But his gnawing problem had still not been settled. Caroline was still Queen Consort of England, and was already asking her advisers what arrangements were being made for her at the Coronation.

Because of her arrival in England, and the protracted battle in the House of Lords, the ceremony had already been postponed from its original intended date. Now it was ordained that it should take place in Westminster Abbey on 19th July 1821, preceded by a great banquet in Westminster Hall.

Queen Caroline declared her intention of being present.

The Privy Council ruled that there was no precept entitling a Queen Consort to be crowned at any specific time, so that if the King did not wish his spouse to be so crowned, she had no traditional claim otherwise.

In that case, Caroline retorted, she should at least have a place at the ceremony, and she asked what procedure she should follow. She was hastily told that the King had not invited her.

Then she would come in her own right.

On the afternoon of 19th July, Queen Caroline arrived at the Abbey in as great a state as she had arrived at the House of Lords on so many dramatic days. She requested admittance at one door, to be told that only ticket-holders could be allowed in. At another door she received the same reply. A companion offered her a ticket, but she refused it: she required entry as of Royal prerogative.

Now she heard shouts she had never expected to hear.

'Shame on you! Go away – go on, off with you!'

The mob which had once roared its approval was turning against her. Months of talk about the results of her trial had left an unpleasant, lingering taste. The acquittal had been no true acquittal, and, however badly she had been treated, most people on sober reflection had come round to the view that her own conduct could hardly have been worse. The King's instigation of pageantry, village festivities and firework displays had brought some colour into a drab and disturbed country. Seen in harsh daylight, vulgarly clamouring outside the holy place where so many English kings had been crowned and so many lay buried, the Queen showed up as a dowdy, dissolute creature not worthy of admittance.

'Shame!'

'Go back to Italy.'

Do go away at any rate . . .

Caroline surrendered, and turned away.

Just under three weeks later, while soliciting sympathetic applause in a box at Drury Lane, she had a sudden inflammation of the bowels, and a few days later was dead.

'I never committed adultery but with one man,' she had once said unblinkingly to a friend, 'and that with the husband of Mrs Fitzherbert.'

The King, just reaching Ireland at the beginning of a tour of his realm, observed a becoming mourning for a decent period. But however black the band on his arm, and however correct the phrases of regret he uttered, in his heart there could be only rejoicing. And perhaps a spice of hatred to add flavour: anger that he should have had to wait so long, that he was growing older and monstrously fat and weary of so much that had once delighted him. If only he might have been free of her years ago!

He devoted himself now to his artistic fancies and fantasies, especially at Brighton, where he saw harbingers of a new age which would follow his own: gas lighting in the Pavilion grounds and then for the chandeliers within. He could pride himself that he had assembled for the nation one of the world's greatest art collections, and encouraged some of its greatest architecture. He hoped future generations would appreciate this, as his own contemporaries so ungratefully failed to do.

In 1830 King George IV was at Windsor when his body began to swell even more grossly than before, and his doctors punctured the soles of his feet in order to draw off great quantities of water. His heart weakened. In June a blood vessel in his stomach burst, and he died.

He was, declared the Duke of Wellington, 'the most extraordinary compound of talent, wit, buffoonery, obstinacy and good feelings, in short, a medley of the most opposite qualities, with a great preponderance of good, that I ever saw in any character in my life.'

On his deathbed the King had received a letter from Maria Fitzherbert, warned by his doctor of what was likely to happen. A week later she received from King William IV, once Duke of Clarence, a number of her portraits which George had always cherished. One which was not, however, returned was an especially beautiful miniature of her set in diamonds. It was some time before she was told that George had worn it about his neck through all the years of their separation, was wearing it at the time of his death, and had given instructions that it was to be buried with him.

In 1837 Maria Fitzherbert died and was buried in the church of St John the Baptist at Brighton. Her memorial shows three wedding rings on her left hand.

Victoria Holt also writes as *Jean Plaidy*

'One of England's foremost historical novelists.'
Birmingham Mail

MURDER MOST ROYAL
A HEALTH UNTO HIS MAJESTY
THE HAUNTED SISTERS
ST THOMAS'S EVE
GAY LORD ROBERT
THE CAPTIVE QUEEN OF SCOTS
HERE LIES OUR SOVEREIGN LORD
THE PRINCE AND THE QUAKERESS
THE WANDERING PRINCE
THE THIRD GEORGE
THE PRINCESS OF CELLE
QUEEN IN WAITING
THE THISTLE AND THE ROSE
THE SIXTH WIFE
THE QUEEN'S FAVOURITES
THE SPANISH BRIDEGROOM
ROYAL ROAD TO FOTHERINGAY
MURDER IN THE TOWER
THE HEART OF THE LION
THE PLANTAGENET PRELUDE

All available in Pan Books